MW01701644

G Street Chronicles
Presents:

Pay Attention To the Red Flags

Self-Esteem Guide

Charlene Davis, BSW, MSW

Published by G Street Chronicles

Library of Congress Control Number: 2010939164
ISBN: 9780982654378

Pay Attention to the Red Flags
Written by: Charlene Davis, BSW, MSW
Text Formation: Write On Promotions

Published by
GStreetChronicles
P.O.Box22
DublinGa.31040
www.gstreetchronicles.com

Acknowledgments

Self-talk produced positive changes in my emotions and my behaviors. To be sure that my greatest achievement was accomplished, I had to first create in my mind the possibility of writing this book. Otherwise, it would have been impossible and unreachable. Don't ever underestimate the power of love.

When you receive support from those who believe in your capabilities, you are able to reach your highest level. To my daughter, Delicia Jones, you have been a great inspiration. You've enhanced my self-confidence. Thank you Dee for giving me my first one hundred dollars to help me self-publish. You've always encouraged me to believe in myself. To my son, Leroy Jones Junior, you have been my stronghold. You've inspired me to be the best. Your encouraging words have helped me to focus on my strengths. You have always made me feel valued.

Pay Attention to the Red Flags

Introduction

Red flags wave in the wind so that women can get a glimpse of trouble in their relationship. Not paying attention to the red flags is the problem that we women face today. The crucial moment is in the beginning of the relationship. If a man shows interest and suddenly finds every excuse to spend time away from you, most likely he is spending time with someone else. We have a desire for love and affection, and we want to be loved by a good man, but not just any man. Being alone and happy is more important than being miserable with someone who does not respect and love you. At dinner, if he always order his meal first, pay attention; he may not be a thoughtful man. When your company comes over, and he sits in the living room, pay attention, he may not be social. At holidays, if he wants to see his parents and never spend time with yours, he may be inconsiderate. Red flags are your warning signs about a failing relationship.

Stop pushing the red flags down with excuses. Do not compromise your needs and desires. If you want a man to massage your feet after a long day at work or cook you a decent meal, do not settle for anything less. He is out there; you have to find him. Stop being a target for a man's emotions. Men will lead you to believe that you are insufficient. Arrogant men and disdainful types tend to frown because they think women are below them. We need to wait, and the right man will come along. It may take a while, so be patient. Just go with the flow. Do not get derailed from the plan of God.

Do not focus on your hurts. Focus on what God told you to do. Stick with your plan to go back to college, start your own business, volunteer at the homeless shelter, build your own church, or open your counseling center. Do things for yourself. If it is your vision, see it to the end.

Forward

On numerous occasions, women date men who they know are dishonest, abusive, and unfaithful. Yet, they remain in the unhealthy relationship. Why do they stay? Not realizing that they are suffering from low self-esteem, they convince themselves that it is the man with the problem. One woman said that she took a long look in the mirror. The conversation went like this: "Do you love yourself? If so, why are you eating the scrap from the table of men who do not have any respect for you?" She never answered her own question. A woman who loves herself will not be afraid to leave a relationship that is unhealthy.

There are compassionate, loyal, and dedicated men in society. We have to know where they are and how to identify them. Men who are controlling have low self-esteem. No one is perfect, but everyone desires to be loved and respected. When we tolerate the abuse, we make it really hard for the next woman. Find the strength within yourself to end an abusive relationship. Stop thinking about how good sex is, do not fear being alone, and respect yourself. Get rid of the old stuff. Start fresh, and seek those men who want the best for you.

Contents

- Listen Without Interrupting Your Man
- Be Loyal to Yourself
- Negativity
- Take Yourself Off the Market
- Promiscuity with Different Men All Over Agai
- Take Your Time
- How to Avoid Becoming Too Emotionally Involved
- Positive Thinker
- Moving On After a Breakup
- Bad-mouthing the Parent
- Pitfalls for Women
- Does He Treat You Like a Queen?
- If You Are Paying His Bills, Tell Him to Head for the Hills
- Is He Ready for Marriage and the Baby Carriage?
- Can You Be Friends with Your Ex?
- Feeling Used and Abused
- Slow Down On Giving Up the Honey
- Don't Do Anything that You Can't Get Into
- Accept Only the Best
- Stop Being Desperate
- Let Him Do the Calling
- Stop Signing Up with Men who Have Nothing to Offer
- Is He Chipping Away at Your Healthy Self-esteem?
- Free Your Mind
- Know When to Be Quiet
- Suffering in Silence
- Benefit of Therapy
- Flooding with Anxiety
- Stupid Behaviors, but Planning to Recover
- When You Learn from the Past, You Make Better Choices in the Future

- Feeling Inadequate
- Struggling to Hide Low Self-esteem
- Moving Forward as a Single Parent
- He Changed His Mind about Being Married
- Never Give Up on Yourself
- Preparing Dinner
- Check Him Out First
- Signs of a Needy Person
- Shake Yourself Loose from that Man
- Sex Is the Icing, But It Is Not the Cake
- Tackle the Insecurities Head-on

Saved and Single

After my divorce, I continued to pray and read my Bible. Allow me to share what God revealed to me. God showed me that I am an attractive woman of godly intelligence. I am complete without a mate. He showed me that there is nothing missing from my life just because I do not have a man. He encouraged me to continue to love myself and, more importantly, love the Lord. He told me that when I continue to delight in him, he will give me the desires of my heart. I needed him to remind me of this. I have everything that I need according to his riches and glory. God told me that I am above a ruby's worth, and a gem does not seek—it is *sought.* I know that I am single, and that is all right with me.

After being in prayer, it was revealed that I do not need a romantic relationship at this time in my life. It is not that I oppose having a relationship. It is that I detest codependency. Praise God for vision and wisdom. As a woman, it is not my role to chase after any man. Esther 2:14 reads that I am to *wait* on my king, and when he is delighted in me, he will *call* me by my name.

My Lord does not intend for me to be needy or desperate. I am to be cherished, relished, valued, and honored. God showed me that it is not my responsibility to convince him or convict him of that. My mate will already know it and consistently show it. He will stay on his knees daily not just to adore me, but to praise the Lord for the virtuous woman he has found. I realize that when I am by myself, I am not alone. I actually know what I have coming to me. I am single and saved right now. That is all I need to be. Praise God for his goodness. Bottom line: anyone can get a good hug, but I want to feel the love when a person holds me.

Love is precious, love is kind,
Love will give you peace of mind.
Love is lasting, love is strong, Love
will help you do no wrong.
Love is trusting, love is commitment, Love is
what you put into it.
Love is peace, love is joy,
Love will be there forever more.

No Teeth

Diana is forty years old. Once upon a time, she met Bob in a grocery store near her home. After a brief conversation, they exchanged phone numbers. Diana and Bob talked on the phone for four months. He appeared to be a caring and loving individual. Bob said that he lived in Georgetown. According to him, he owned a five-bedroom house. But he never allowed her to visit. Red flags. He also told her that he owned a hardware store. Before their first date, he described himself as honest and hardworking. Unfortunately, she agreed to go on a date. Bob called Diana two days before their date to warn her about a deficit he has. He claimed he was in a motorcycle accident a while ago, and his front teeth had fallen out. He said that he did not want to show up looking like a crazy person with no teeth. She asked him when the work was going to be done on his teeth, and he said in about six months. Being the kind of person that she is, she met with him anyway. Once face-to-face, he hugged her and smiled.

Trying not to laugh, she noticed that he had one gold tooth hanging in the front of his mouth and one silver tooth on the left side at the bottom.

The rest were pink *gums*. Her heart dropped. She could not believe that an adult man would show up on a date in that condition. Diana did not notice that his teeth were missing in the store because she was in a hurry the day that they met. At dinner, he smiled the whole time. During the interview, Diana said, "It was so hard looking into his face." Thoughts ran through her mind. Diana contemplated excusing herself to go to the bathroom, leaving out the side door, and never returning to the table.

But she stayed. Her inside started to hurt because she was holding back her laugh. The waiter kept looking at her as if he felt sorry for her. Minutes later, Bob excused himself to use his cell phone in private. A tall man with a navy blue suit, brown eyes, and a smile to die for got up out of his seat and walked toward Diana. He said, "Miss, excuse me for interrupting. May I ask you a personal question?" Diana said, "Yes." He said, "Why in the hell are you sitting with that no-teeth guy? You are so pretty, and you deserve better."

Then he walked away. The next day, Diana decided to drive to Bob's house in Georgetown. She found out that he does not own a home or business. He lives with his schizophrenic mother, alcoholic brother, two drug-abused, unemployed sisters, a hamster, a black and white cat, and his *wife*. Immediately, she ended the relationship. He never got those damn teeth. The red flags were all there, and she kept pushing them down.

Men 101

If you ask him a simple question and he gets upset, pay attention: he is guilty of something. Do your research and ask questions to find out as much as possible before you have sex with him or say "I do." On Valentine's Day, if you see him in the morning, and then in the evening you cannot locate him, he may be spending time with someone else. If he calls to come over but claims that he does not have any gas money, pay attention: he wants you to come get him. Then you will be buying him gas for the month. When it is time to pay rent on the first and he picks an argument with you at the end of the month, pay attention: he is trying to get out of paying the rent. Women, have you ever been constantly called another woman's name?

Pay attention: maybe he is involved with that person. When he goes into the bathroom with his cell phone for hours, he is definitely hiding something. If he is wearing new outfits each week, yet he is crying broke, most likely someone is buying his clothes. Ladies, do not let your denial be deeper than your grave. Your silence is not going to rescue you. Ask the man if there has been a change in your relationship. Some men have a problem establishing intimate relationships with a woman because they fear losing their autonomy.

Blinded by Love

Ashley Smith was born in Orange County, California. Ashley was raised in an abusive environment. She witnessed her father drinking and fighting with her mother on weekends.

Although the abuse was not directly toward Ashley, she remembers ducking a flying chair that hit her mother in the face, and blood smeared over the bedroom wall. On another occasion, the police arrested Ashley's father for cutting her mother's left hand of because dinner was not ready when he arrived home from work. Ashley told her girlfriends that she would never date an abusive man.

She appeared to be timid, unsure of herself, weary, and gloomy. For most of Ashley's adult life, she wore slip-on shoes and braids, and her makeup was a natural light tan color. Ashley decided to go to her high school prom with the football quarterback. On prom night, Jason arrived in a white limousine to pick her up for the prom. He was dressed in a black tuxedo, shinning cuff links, and a silk bow tie. His hair was dark brown, he was six-two, and he had blue eyes. When he pulled up in front of her house, he asked the driver to blow the horn. Pay attention. A man who is interested in you will come to the door and knock.

Ashley kneeled on the couch to peep out the living room window, almost tripping over the long cream-colored dress that she was wearing. Eventually, the doorbell rang, and her little sister hurried to the door to let Jason in. As she led him to the family room, Ashley rushed downstairs to the powder room to wipe the sweat of her face.

Approaching the room where Jason was waiting, Ashley's heart skipped two beats. It was her first date with a man, and she was not sure what to expect. Jason stood up as she entered the room. He appeared to be amazed at the beautiful woman standing in front of him. As he reached for her right hand, he gently kissed it and placed it back in position. Ashley glared into his dark brown eyes, and she felt herself about to faint. *Stay with me,* a small voice in her head replied. *Don't lose your cool. He is just a man.*

Then, a smile appeared on her face. It took about three seconds before she could speak. "Are you okay?" he asked.

"Yes, I am just excited about the prom."

"We will have a ball. I have heard so many great things about you, Ashley, and I am looking forward to getting to know you."

"Are you sure you are talking about me?" That was the first sign of low self-esteem. Ashley did not know how to accept a compliment. "I am an ordinary woman," she replied. "Most of my time has been spent at home in my room curled up reading a good book. Dating has been the furthest thing from my mind."

After entering the ballroom, her friends came over to meet and greet her new man. One woman whispered in Ashley's ear, and she told her that Jason was no good. "He hates women, and he physically abused me when we were dating."

However, Ashley thought that the girl was jealous of their relationship. Another woman who was on the cheerleading team told Ashley that Jason was a player, and he would break her heart. When Ashley confronted Jason about these comments, he told Ashley that those women were mad because he rejected them. Ashley reached out and took Jason by his right hand. "May I have the first dance?"

"Yes, you may, my first lady."

The band began to play a nice melody. Ashley lifted her long dress, and she glided across the marble floor. When the dance was over, Jason offered to get her a drink of punch. "Let me go with you."

"No, you stay here and look beautiful." Within minutes, he returned to where she had found a cozy seat in the corner of the dance floor. Ashley sipped the drink slowly. She seemed to be more relaxed.

"So, Jason, tell me a little about you. Are you involved with anyone special?"

"No, I am too busy trying to decide what college I am

going to attend in the spring."What about you? Is there a guy that you daydream about?"

"Of course not, I am waiting on you."

"Oh my goodness, where did that come from?" She could not believe those words came out of her mouth. It was obvious that the punch was spiked. They decided to dance with each other all night. When the clock struck midnight, Jason collected Ashley, and they headed for the limo waiting in front of the door. Jason dropped Ashley of at home, kissed her slightly on the lips, and road of in the limo.

Three weeks later, he was constantly on her mind. So she broke down and called him. After dating for six months, they fell in love and got married. Both of them completed college and moved to Atlanta, Georgia. Ashley got pregnant and had a baby boy. He died a day later from breathing complications. They went through the grieving process. After work, hitting the gym was their outlet, and they met new friends, had parties on weekends, traveled, and enjoyed quality time with each other. After about a year, Ashley noticed that Jason was coming home a little later than usual. When she asked him what was going on at work, he damn near bit her head off. "My job has nothing to do with you."

"Baby, we are married, and I am concerned about you."

"I am not your baby. A baby is what we lost, thank

goodness." He slammed the hall closet door where he hung his suit coat and stormed out onto the deck.

Ashley was a smart woman, and she recognized the signs of a problem. One day, she decided to rent a used car, and she followed Jason when he got off from work. She saw him going down a street unknown to her. He pulled into a parking space and started walking down the street. After following him on foot for two blocks, he stopped in front of a big white house with large windows and a fence surrounding the yard. He looked back as if to make sure he was not being followed. She ducked behind some tall bushes, her long curly hair getting caught on a branch. She yanked hard to get loose, almost pulled her braid out, and fell in the bushes.

Tears streamed down both sides of her face, and the pink blouse that she wore was now brown from the dirt. When the door opened, Ashley saw a young child. "Hi, Daddy," he said. Ashley felt herself get nauseated. She began to vomit. Ashley sat in those bushes for two hours until Jason came out. He had on a different shirt and pants. Then he walked toward his car. She waited until he drove off, and she found a shortcut home. Then she washed up and had dinner on the table when he arrived.

"Hello, Jason," she said in a calm voice. "How was your day?"

"Actually, I had a great day."

"What made it so great?"

"My boss is impressed with the new project that I presented to the board of directors today. Therefore, he took me out for a drink and late lunch. Look at the gift the women bought me at work for helping them get a raise."

"Dinner is ready," she said.

"Ashley, the food smells fantastic, but I am not hungry."

"Jason, I prepared your special meal tonight."

"I will take it for lunch tomorrow." After kissing her on the forehead, he went upstairs and went straight to bed. When she got in bed, he placed his right hand on her breast, caressing her nipple, trying to prepare her for having sex. She pulled away. "I am not in the mood for sex tonight. It is time for my period, and I am cramping badly." He frowned as if he was upset. Ashley turned over and fell asleep.

In the middle of the night, she awoke to a violent man. Jason had crawled on top of her, and he was ripping her gown of. "Stop, Jason, what in the hell are you doing?"

"I am taking what is mine." Then he punched her in the face, tore of her underwear, pulled on her hair, and took two ropes that he had hidden under his pillow, tied her arms to the brass bed rails, and raped her repeatedly. Her frail body was broken into.

"Where did this man come from?" she moaned to herself.

After two hours of being abused, he left her lying in her own blood until morning.

Ashley heard Jason coming out of the shower, and she could barely hold her head up. But she was able to say these words: "Oh my God, my friends were right."

Jason said, "You are crazy as hell, stupid bitch. You should have listened to what those heifers had to say. I hate all women. Did one of them tell you that I broke her nose and knocked out both of her front teeth?"

"Yes, I was told that story." Carrie had told her that she was five months pregnant and on the way back home one night from dinner with Jason when he pulled into a dark alley, took a baseball bat, beat her in her stomach until she started to bleed, and the baby died. Carrie told Jason, "I must be insane. I still love you. If I do not see you again, I will certainly lose my mind. If I never hear you say I love you again, my life ends." He left her there to die. A drunken man found her lying next to a dumpster surrounded by rats and garbage. She was left there to die, but she was still breathing. The police were called. Jason was arrested and hauled off to jail. His father was rich, and he bribed the judge. He got out in an hour. "That bitch is finally out of my life to," he said out loud. She did not pay attention to the red flags.

Warning Signs

Decreased Sexual Passion

There is a natural waxing and waning of passion that happens in some relationships, but what I am speaking about here is something else. While stress, fatigue, loss of employment, constant disappointments and other pressures can slide between the sheets, there is no place for rage at anytime. A man is not showing you love if he is abusing you physically, mentally, financially or emotionally.

Fussing

When a couple argues most of the time, it has become a bad habit. Although it does not bother them, it is embarrassing in the presence of family, co-workers and friends. In order for your love to remain promising and healthy, you have to be able to have discussions about both small and complex feelings. When arguing replaces discussions, nothing gets nothing gets resolved. Instead, tension builds and a power battle takes over.

Then, the relationship goes sour. After a while, anger, abuse, and blame follow. Do not waste time on conversations that are not beneficial to building a healthy relationship with anyone. Like it or not, straight talk is healthy. Without it, you will lose your boundaries and values. We all have to stand up for something even when it is not accepted the way we expect. Real differences in a partnership do not have to cause problems, unless we make it a problem especially when they are explored with respect. When you remain silent and stoic and keep everything beneath the surface, repressed feelings become part of a toxic brew. Eventually they take on a life of their own, and the relationship is destroyed.

You have to be careful about this warning sign called Jealousy. It's confusing. Jealousy is a difficult emotion. It can mean several things. The type of jealousy that I am referring to is unfounded jealousy, not jealousy that comes from watching a flirtatious husband or significant other about to make a conquest. Unfounded jealousy is something that shows up without warning signs and disturbs the balance of a relationship. This type of jealousy appears out of nowhere and can have little to do with infidelity. It is a reflection of your or your significant other's insecurity and low self-esteem. This type of jealousy causes women and men to behave in a destructive or abusive manner toward each other.

Little Time Spent Together

When is enough time together enough? Well, that all depends on your actual needs. Locating the balance between other commitments creates a continuous juggling act. We all have experienced that. But, an abrupt shift in shared time patterns could be a red flag that something is out of whack in the relationship.

Too much separation and not enough shared time can develop a void, making intimacy difficult to experience. Time spent apart will become a habit, and a wedge will be drawn between the relationships. If you find that your mate is enjoy being with the men more than with you, that is a red flag. Ask him up front, why is it that you like spending more time with your male friend than with me?

Anxiety

I think of anxiety as a red flag in much the same way that I think of bipolar disorder or depression. A sudden increase in anxiety or a change in normal sleeping habits can be a sign that there is an unresolved issue lurking in your subconscious that needs to be exposed. Relationships are so imperative in life.

There is a big chance that anxiety is a red flag indicating that some aspect of your partnership needs to be examined. For example, you or your mate maybe experiencing excessive worry and fear about something that has occurred in your life. The anxiety can be treated with psychotherapy or supportive therapy. Everyone has problems, and support is available.

Dependency

When you're too dependent, the fundamental partnership is out of balance. If there is too much dependency, a natural resentment is stirred up. These people tend to lack self-confidence, and they are unable to function independently. They rely on others to assume responsibility for them. One person is likely to feel burdened and overwhelmed, the other frightened by his own neediness.

Dependent women are afraid to be alone. This is one reason why they jump from relationship to relationship. No one wins in this situation. Equality is thrown out the window and the front door. It is never recovered. The one in power often feels unappreciated, undervalued, unneeded, unloved and unwanted. The needy one frequently feels disappointment. Resentment grows, and both partners feel criticized

Manipulation of Family Members

When you begin to manipulate and clutch at your children or others, your partner can easily be marginalized. A division can occur. Low-level family warfare can result. This can happen not only with children but with other family members, friends, and even colleagues. The result is that you and your significant other are at odds. Relationships are enormously complex. Sometimes it may feel that it is too late. I have watched relationships blossom.

Most issues can be resolved by honest dialogue and open communication that require you to leave behind all your ammunition. Every relationship fights against an undertow that takes you back to your childhood. Breaking that cycle is fundamental to keeping love fresh and healthy. Dealing with reality is important. Tundra is thirty five years old, fair skin, short black hair and brown eyes. She has been in three abusive relationships in the last five years. She has suffered from physical abuse, mental abuse and sexual abuse. "I would always push down any red flags that appeared, hoping that he would change or it would cease to bother me in the future. It always ended and resulted with hurt."

Women, you must pay close attention to how the relationship is developing. When the cost outweighs the benefits, you know that there is a problem. If he is cold, angry, and starts to blame you for no apparent reason, that is a red flag. The next minute, he will be warm and lovable. These patterns are common in a relationship that is in trouble. Sometimes there is an underlying problem that has not been identified; it may not have anything to do with you for the most part. Or, the person may be insecure. Those on the outside can see well than those on the inside.

You are too tied up in the relationship to recognize that you need some form of help. However, once you realize that there is a problem and you decide to make a change, you procrastinate until a later date. This becomes a bad habit. Paying attention to the red flags will let you know when the boat is about to sink. When the waves are heavy, the boat begins to rock.

Everyone is told to grab their life jacket. Women, you have to learn how to stand while going through troubles. Be aware that when you keep complaining about the same things that have happened to you in the past, you become easy prey for the devil. He will play on your weakness and vulnerability. We know a semicolon stands for two things. The period means stop, and the comma means that something else is coming. So keep your head up, walk in faith, trust God for what you need, and never doubt.

God will turn up the heat to get your attention. He wants us to rely on him and only him. I am sure that at times it seems like your life is over. It is not over. God has the final say. If you feel that you are alone in the world and no one cares about you, take some deep breaths and close your eyes. Imagine that you cannot get up from your seat; you are blind, unable to feed yourself. Focus on your blessings. Stop complaining about what a man has not done or has done to you, and focus on what you can do to help the next woman. Women, put on the whole armor of God. Let your prayers be your shield.

Being Rushed Leads to Unhappiness

Those who feel rushed are less likely to be happy, and those who do not feel rushed are the most likely to be very happy. I think that if women took their time to get to know the man better, they would identify their irreconcilable differences and spare themselves heartaches, disappointments, and pain. When I was a teenager, the thing I wanted most in the whole world was to get married, which was part of my continuing quest to create a healthy family.

I honestly believe marriage is built on love and connection and all that good stuff. As I completed my research, I found that some marriages are built on habit and comfort. As we all know, some relationships that last for years are based on a dysfunctional foundation held together by ten-year apartment leases or a mortgage. Certainly, there are many unmarried people living together for a lot of reasons. In many of these situations, both people are getting exactly what they want and desire. I'm not about to completely knock cohabitation.

We are all different. It's the rushing in that concern me. When your head is clear, you make good judgments. You take your time, you get to know who you are as a person, you know what you expect from a relationship, and you are mature enough to walk away in the event the relationship does not last. Before moving in with someone, be sure where the relationship is headed, never assume anything, and make sure he wants you to move in with him before you decide to move your belongings, and furniture in.

Once you're living together, it can get so difficult to leave, to break up, and to pull your heart away from the relationship. Ending the relationship becomes a life change for both people. The main point is that when you hurry into a relationship, you hurry into a relationship you haven't fully explored and perhaps aren't ready to fully commit to.

Or, your partner may not be ready for a commitment. Taking time allows us to move slowly and surely. The right man will not want to be hurried into a serious relationship. Most single men have been dating other women, and they can easily identify a desperate woman that I am looking to get married. At times, women expect men to be eager to have sex and get married right away. If the man is not eager, she feels that something is wrong with her. Although men enjoy sex, they never want to feel hurried into something that they are not seeking. When a man takes a woman out on a date, he already knows what he expects from her. Women, I am telling you to slow down.

Truth about Men

Any man can father a baby. A real man is a working man and provider for his family. If a man lives at home with his mom, doesn't pay the mortgage, and eats your food instead of providing it, ask you for gas money every week, he is not eligible. If he wants you to work, pay his bills, pay tuition fees, pay his car note, buy the food, pay the gas bill, pay the mortgage while he goes to college, and never get a job on spring break that is a red flag.

A true man will produce promising results. If he does not have his own car, and you are paying his bus fare, get rid of him. If he does not spend time doing things that you enjoy, he is selfish. If he asks you for money often, he is broke Women, pay attention to the red flags. You are marvelous. Men who constantly think of their own pleasures and interests will make you yield to them. They will make you feel that you are blest to have them as your mate.

These men are never satisfied, and they cannot seem to find happiness within themselves. When parents put these men on a pedestal at a young age, they create spoiled, selfish human beings. This selfishness grows more dominant the older a man becomes. For some reason, these men assume that the world owes them everything. Only what they desire is important, and your wants are put on the back burner. They lack empathy; they are unwilling to identify the needs of others. They want to be treated as though they are SUPERIOR and KINGS, without any measurable achievements. Make note, men who honor and respect their parents, especially their mom, will respect you as well. Women who are in bad relationships with these types of men want to tell their friends, family, and co-workers about how they are being treated. But their partner's threatening glare reminds them it would be safer to keep their mouth shut and deal with it.

Melissa Gilmore is a heavyset African American female. She is five-two, weighs 220 pounds, straight long black hair, a beautiful smile, white teeth, big breast and a baby doll face. She was married for about three years. Melissa had a baby with her husband Hun, and they appeared to be a happy couple. All of a sudden, her Hun no longer wanted to have sex because he claimed that he did not want to take the risk of her getting pregnant again.

When she offered to take birth control pills, Hun made up an excuse. He led her to believe that he was worried about her health due to the side effects of birth control pills. Then, she asked Hun to use a condom, and he said, “If I cannot have sex naturally, I will just do without. I will not have sex until you get your tubes tied. I do not want anymore children.” Melissa wanted more children. So, she refuses to get her tubes tied.

During the Christmas holiday, she went shopping with her mother. They were supposed to be gone all day. After walking in 3 inch heels for two hours, her feet could no longer stand the burning pain in the bottom of her feet. So, she drove home. As she reached the house, there was a yellow hummer parked in her driveway. Her mother helped her take the bags into the house.

As they entered the house, Melissa's eyes glared at the white mink fur that was neatly laid across the living room sofa. As she quietly picked up the fur, she read the name inside the coat. Sue Anne Golden. She thought to herself, *Who in the hell is Sue Anne Golden?* "Come with me mom." She said. Her mother walked close behind her as they walked up thirteen wooden stairs. As she reached the bedroom, the floor cracked, and the door was open enough wherefore; she could see inside.

Melissa eased her head in, and her hair fell in her face. She saw two people who were obviously enjoying oral sex. Melissa heard her teeth gritting against each other, her heart was pushing to come through her chest, her face was red, and she was in a rage. In the hall closet, a bottle of baby oil was sitting on the top shelf. She unscrewed the top, poured the oil on the magnolia floor in the bathroom, eased back toward the guest room which is across from her bedroom, and she waited. She overhead her Hun telling the woman that he wanted them to take a shower together.

As he entered the bathroom without turning on the light, put his right foot forward, and down he went. He hit the right side of his temple against the sharp edge of the cabinet sink. Blood was gushing out fast. The woman screamed, and she went to his aid. Melissa crept up behind her, took the black shinny .357 gun that was tucked away in the draw in the guest room, blew the woman's head of, and shot her Hun in the chest three times.

Melissa left them in the bathroom, locked the bedroom door from the outside, drove about a mile to the corner store, and chatted with the cashier which is a tall slim lady with blonde hair. After thirty minutes, she arrived back home. Melissa's mother called the police to report that there was a strange car in the driveway. The police instructed her mother to leave the house.

Once the police arrived, they found the woman and Hun scattered all over the bathroom. After a thorough investigation was done, Melissa was charged with first-degree murder because her diamond earring was found next to Hun. She told the police during the investigation that she had never been near neither of them. Melissa is serving twenty years in prison for the murder of Hun and his lover which was his best friends' wife.

Jasmine Zody had been married for about five years. She used Andy's car to go shopping, and she came back home. Her husband went to work, and she remembered that she left a pair of new shoes in the car. She went to his job and got the shoes out of the trunk. To her surprise, there was a pair of women's underwear and a new outfit sizes six in the trunk. She wore a size 10. She approached Andy, and he said, "I do not know where those things came from." Then she threw them at him, and he said, "Don't mess up those underwear and outfit" They argued for about ten minutes in front of his place of employment. Then, he took his fist and punched her in the face, blacking her left eye. After several punches, she told him that she was sorry for not trusting him.

When he arrived home that evening, he brought her two dozen red roses and made passionate love to her. Pay attention women. Any man who hits you does not love you. If you think that your friend or love one is being abused, ask them some leading questions. Ask them to describe their situation in detail and observe their behavior. If you show that you understand them, they will have the willingness to discuss their situation in details. That way, you can offer to support them to seek the help that they need, and achieve their goal to get out.

Cynthia had been dating Bob for about six and a half years. They were planning to get married. He had a key to her apartment. However, she did not have a key to his house. She dropped by her man's house unexpectedly, and his car was in the driveway. After knocking for fifteen minutes, he came to the door, and he appeared shocked to see her standing there. His mouth was open wide, and he was sweating. Bob's head was out the door, and his left foot was blocking her from entering. Bob made an excuse not to let Cynthia inside, so she left. She thought to herself, "There is a woman inside."

At 7:00 pm, she called Bob's house, and he answered, and he claimed to be sleeping. "Are you in for the night?" "Yes," he said. She and a girlfriend decided to go eat at Friday's restaurant in Annapolis, Maryland. Lo and behold, she heard a voice that sounded familiar. "It can't be him," she said to herself. She peeped over into the other booth, and there her man was with another woman.

They were sitting as close as two peas in a pot. He had a beautiful diamond ring in his hand, and he was telling the woman how much he loved her. Cynthia's heart was beating fast, and it was trying to come through shirt. Her blood pressure was rising, and her skin was flushed. Cynthia took deep breaths and spoke in a low tone. She asked her friend to order their meal. She waited patiently.

After her man ate his meal, she watched him leave the restaurant. Twenty minutes later, Cynthia called his cell phone, and it went to voice mail. Cynthia took of her heels, and she walked outside. She saw her man snuggling in a corner on the side of the building with the woman. She watched them kissing for a few minutes.

When they finished kissing, he lead her to the passenger side of his truck, opened the door, and she climbed in. They drove off. About 10:30 pm, Cynthia called the house and cell phone, but there was no answer. She drove by his house, and his truck was in the driveway. The next day, she asked him about his night. "My night was fantastic," he responded. She was crying on the inside, but she did not say a word. The next day, she changed the locks on her door, home and cell phone numbers cancelled his charge cards for which she was paying bills, had his truck picked up, put it back in her driveway which was in her name, and she was paying the payments. Immediately, she ended the relationship.

Women, although it may be painful to leave a relationship that you have been invested in for years, you must love yourselves enough to move on. The importance of establishing meaningful and healthy relationships cannot be overemphasized. A relationship is not healthy if you are paying all his bills.

Mercedes Hall had been married to her husband for twenty-two years. During the night, she worked as a registered nurse. Her demented mother lived with her and Eric. Mercedes refused to put her mom in a nursing home. One day, Mercedes came home from work, and her mother appeared delusional. She told Mercedes that Eric had another woman in the house. Mercedes shared this information with Eric, and they both laughed. The mother overheard their conversation, and she became combative.

She threw a plate at Eric, and cursed him. Mercedes called the doctor, and he recommended that the patient be taken to the emergency room. Once she was evaluated, it was determined that her mother's dementia had gotten worse.

Two years later, Mercedes left work early because she had a stomach virus. Her mother was sound asleep. When Mercedes drove up, she noticed a blue 2000 Lexus in her driveway. Of course, her mind began to race. It was 2:30 am. She eased her key into the lock; she heard a murmuring sound coming from her first-floor bedroom. Entering the house, she tripped over her shoelace that had become untied. She almost fell. Mercedes was five-six, with long blonde hair, hazel eyes, and fair skin.

As she slowly walked down the short hallway, the murmuring got louder. Since it was dark, it was difficult to see ahead of her. Reaching into the desk drawer that was located to the right of the staircase, she retrieved a flashlight and continued to walk toward the bedroom. Once she reached the entrance, she noticed a night-light on. Two images were moving up and down in the shadow.

There were moaning and groaning going on. When she turned on the light, to her surprise, Mercedes's best friend Sally was having sex with Eric. Sally had moved in with Mercedes because

Sally's husband had cheated on her with Sally's sister two months ago. After the breakup, Sally was heartbroken, and she missed work for weeks and got fired. In the middle of the night, she called Mercedes from the bus station. Mercedes drove eighty-two miles to pick Sally up. Mercedes loaned Sally money, bought her clothes, provided food, let her borrow the car, and gave her access to her checking account.

Sally got comfortable, and she decided to take a piece of Eric. Mercedes packed her bags, took her mother, changed her bank account, and left the house that night. Starting fresh, she never looked back. The court made Sally pay alimony. Sally is living one day at a time. Women, never move a female friend into your home. If you want to be helpful, pay her hotel bill, buy her some McDonald's food and call it a day.

How to Identify a Healthy Relationship

Healthy relationships are fun and make you feel good about yourself. We can have a healthy relationship with anyone in our life, including your family, friends, and dating partners. Relationships take time, energy, and care to make them healthy. The relationships that you make in your teen years will be a special part of your life and will teach you some of the most important lessons about who you are.

This guide will help you understand different kinds of relationships, what makes each relationship special, and how to communicate in a positive way. I have included common stories and fun ways to work on many kinds of relationships. Communication and sharing are the most important parts of any healthy relationship between two people. By talking and listening to one another, you and the other person can figure out what your common interests are. You can share your feelings with the other person and trust that person will be there to listen and support you. In healthy relationships, people don't lie.

Communication is based on honesty and trust. By listening carefully and sharing your thoughts and feelings with another person, such as a man, you show him that he is an important part of your life.

Respect and Trust

In healthy relationships, you learn to respect and trust important people in your life. Disagreements may still happen, but you learn to stay calm and talk about how you feel. Talking calmly helps you to understand the real reason for not getting along, and it's much easier to figure out how to fix the problem. In healthy relationships, working through disagreements often makes the relationship stronger. In a healthy relationship, people respect each other for who they are. You must respect and listen to yourself and your feelings so you can set boundaries and feel comfortable. You will find that you learn to understand the experiences and feelings of others, and they understand your experiences and feelings.

You know that you are in a healthy relationship with someone because you feel good about yourself when you are with that person. Unhealthy relationships can make you feel sad, angry, or fearful. Healthy peer relationships involve an equal amount of give and take in the relationship. In unhealthy relationships, there is unbalance. You may feel that most of the time you give the other person more attention then he gives to you.

You should feel safe around the other person and feel that you can trust each other with your secrets. In a healthy relationship, you like to spend time with the other person, instead of feeling like you're pressured into spending time with him. Unhealthy relationships do not include trust and respect, which are very important parts of a family relationship, good friendship, or dating relationship.

Healthy dating relationships should start with the same ingredients that healthy friendships have, such as good communication, honesty, and respect. Dating relationships are a little different because they may include physical affection, like hugging, kissing, or holding hands. As with all relationships, it may be tempting at first for you to spend all of your time with your new partner. But making special time to spend together and apart means that you will be able to work on having a healthy relationship with the person you are dating and with other people in your life, like your friends, family, or co-workers.

Never allow anyone to pressure you to do something that you do not want to do. Men must respect your right to say no to anything that makes you feel uncomfortable. It is imperative that you are both clear with each other about your values and your limits. By talking about how each of you feel about a lot of things, you may avoid getting into situations where you are pressured into making a decision on the spot about something very important.

Tips

- Get to know a person by talking on the phone or at work before you go out with him for the first time. Go out with friends to a public place or restaurant the first few times.
- Plan an activity, like going to the movies or picnic.
- Be clear with the other person about what you feel comfortable doing.
- Tell at least one family member where you are going, who you will be with, and how to reach you.
- Dating relationships can be a fun and exciting part of your life. They may be a little confusing, especially if dating is new to you. Once you know that the person you like likes you too, you might be unsure of what to do next. You can start by learning about what makes a dating relationship healthy.

The most important thing to remember is to stay safe, especially when you begin to date. Continue to surround yourself with people who encourage you to be your best self. Read a motivational book for fifteen minutes each day or listen to some CD's. When dealing with chronically negative people, it is important to set strong boundaries; protect yourself by sending a message to them that you care enough about yourself to avoid negativity. Instead of saying how you can't do something, strive toward finding ways that you can.

A positive attitude rubs of, and people will continue to notice. The same is true if you are negative, and no one likes being around someone negative. You are awesome, intelligent, and fun to be around. I am so proud of you for taking time to read this book to get the help you need. Being an inspiration to you brings me pleasure. Having balance is the key to show people that you refuse to put up with their crap.

Dating Is Collecting Data

Gathering information ensures that you identify a dysfunctional man. A man who exhibits conflict, misbehavior, and continual abuse is subject to have those same behaviors in a new relationship. Those individuals tend to believe that this type of behavior is normal or healthy. Some of the causes a dysfunctional man is due to alcohol and drug abuse of the parents that have reared thc children who are now adults.

However, collecting too much information in the early stage of the relationship can be a bad thing, because in the beginning insecurities are high. Therefore, let the relationship move into a more solid territory before getting into the past, and keep it short. It is important to keep the lines of communication open. Everyone wants to know that they are well loved. Respect the person who you are right now. Be proud of who you are, and stay focused on your goals.

Wasting Time on the Wrong Man

Some women may date a loser for years even though they realize that the man is not meeting their needs. Time is of the essence. Wasting time on a loser is not healthy for anyone. Identify the differences between a healthy relationship and an unhealthy relationship. Love is true and pure, and there is no in-between. If you find yourself questioning whether he is the one, trust your instinct, he is not the man for you. Stop wasting so much precious time. A relationship is better when it is shared with the right person.

For example, you have been dating the same guy for over fifteen years, and you decide that you are ready to settle down. He is talking about buying a new car, and he never mentions a ring. Trust me; he is not thinking about marrying you. Just move on. His mind is on other things, and you are not his first priority. I would contend that if you are having fun, you are not wasting your time.

There are a lot of people who are married and miserable. Just because a woman is single does not mean that she does not love men. In order to have healthy relationships with men, you have to have a healthy mindset. Women need to learn that careers and moneymaking are more important goals than bad

relationships involving codependency, drugs, sexual, verbal, physical, and emotional abuse. I ask you, where can a relationship go if you haven't already established who you are, where you're going, and how you're going to get there? You've got to know what you're looking for in a mate, and then find him or her.
If you are in a relationship, you might feel guilty for not being able to leave. Your friends may get fed up with you for being so stuck and dependent. Even your therapist could lose patience.

You feel judged, weak and ashamed of yourself. The abuser is smart. He tells the abused that he loves her. She needs to hear those three words to feel good about her. She becomes like a rat in a tiny cage. People who suffer from low self- esteem are victims in their own homes. They are so confused about what is right and have no knowledge regarding what is wrong. In most instances, the person is abusive to him and others, enjoys drama, looks for problems, can't enjoy happiness, and spends time with those individuals who offer pity and support. For the most part, they hide their feelings well, never want to receive positive advice because they are fixated on negative thoughts.

Once a relationship is over, it needs to end immediately. No one really strives to be in an unhealthy relationship because they all know that each day may be their last one. Being blinded by the views of others is the worst thing. It is imperative that the world know that women are alive and emotionally available. Examine yourself, and love who you are at the moment. Battered women need someone to empathize with them and show genuine concern. I am striving to help you identify your positive characteristics by focusing on your strengths. Stay away from men who are not supportive and caring. Present yourself in the most confident manner, and never take your eyes off of yourself. Keep the frown away, and look into the mirror to glorify the beauty that is inside of you. Motivate yourself to take long drives or watch a movie at home with friends who are supportive. Avoiding negative people is the first step to reaching another level of success. It is no one's fault if we fail. Staying in line with the spirit is the best source of strength. You are an intelligent individual, and trust that you will succeed. Stick with the basics, and connect with those people who think highly of you and want to see you grow. Allow yourself to laugh and find humor in the simplest things.

Keep smiling. Never doubt yourself. Remember, it starts with a positive attitude. It is important to associate with those friends who are true and loyal to you. Avoid those people who intentionally disappoint you. Hang around friends who make you laugh and who you can learn from. Friends will help you become a better person. A good friend is one that has a bond that no one can break. Learn from your experiences, but do not hold onto them. Value your opinions, learn to cope with loss, do not be afraid to be alone, and a true man will find you.

Friends

Friends are precious, kind, and true.
I have never had a friend like you.
I have never had a friend in the past.
So, this is a friendship that I pray will last.

By Charlene Davis, MSW

The greatest people in the world are those who don't know it, and I am telling you that you are one of those great people. In this life, God gives grace to the humble but resists the proud. I asked God to keep me humble because I want to be pleasing in his sight. You are one of God's favorite angels, and he will forever see favor in you. Just remember, clothing makes neither a woman nor a man; it merely reflects the person within. We are a reflection of God's handiwork, and we must remember that at all times.

You are a divine vessel of God. As we continue to live, we need to guard our heart and mind against all negative and unhealthy associations. It is okay to welcome moments of solitude, and we can make them our friend. Let's take the time to silence all noises that could distract us from the still, small voice of God. You can rejoice in the fact that you are not superwoman.

However, you are a terrific woman. Start to empower others by seeking their assistance. Strive to live a balanced life in spite of your many obligations. No one deserves it more than you. Build rest time into your calendar along with your duties to keep your life balance. Remember, Rome was not built in a day. If it is a nice day, go out, and let the breeze blow through your hair. We all need love that we can see. True love eliminates doubt, and it is consistent, which gives a sense of security. Show me a man who is fine, and I will choose true love, loyalty, and commitment every time. When a relationship ends, you will miss him, and forgetting him may be hard, but you must let him go. The reality of life is that no one is above starting fresh.

With the right mind-set, you will exam your thought process and make a better choice next time.

Betrayal

Vanessa was fifty years old when she met Bob at a party. They hit it off right away. They both wanted to know each other better. He sent her flowers at work, and they decided to date for a while. After two years, he proposed. Six months later, they got married. Five years into the marriage, he was served court papers at their home for child support, and he hid the papers from Vanessa for months.

Finally, the judge put a warrant out for his arrest. The sheriff came to the home at 2:00 am, and Vanessa answered the door. Bob heard them talking, and he hid in the garage. The sheriff found him, and he was arrested. On the day of court, he begged Vanessa not to come. She showed up anyway to offer him support. The judge announced that he was being sued for child support, and he owed back pay for seven years. Vanessa was overwhelmed because she did not know that Bob had any children.

She insisted that he get a DNA test done. The results proved that he was the father of two beautiful twin girls. Vanessa was blown away. He never told Vanessa about the girls. Now they fuss all the time, and she eavesdrops on his phone calls because she has lost faith in him. Although she is not happy living with him, she has lost the desire to start over. Women, raise your standards to a higher level. Pay attention to the red flags. At Christmas time, Bob was always broke because he was buying gifts for his girls, and he mailed them to New York. He never kept his wallet on the dresser, slept with it under his pillow, eliminated caller ID, stopped visiting his family members, and never introduced Vanessa to his old friends. He was afraid that she would stumble onto the truth. After five more years, he divorced Vanessa, disappeared out of her life, and married the woman who had his twins.

Vanessa tried to commit suicide. She is now in therapy, and the therapist is trying to make her comfortable. Vanessa has gone through training, and she attends support groups. The goal is to promote mental resilience through optimism. She has been educated on the risk factors of suicide and how to identify the warning signs.

Monica was twenty-four years old when she met Stephen. They met in the cafeteria line at work as she was fixing her salad. As she approached the soda fountain, they both made eye contact. He smiled, and she responded with a slight grin. She pushed her way through the crowd to find a seat in the corner that was her favorite spot. *Wow, alone at last,* she thought to herself. Little did she know Stephen was checking her out because he really wanted to get to know her. He spotted her in the corner, and she motioned to him to come over. Before sitting down, he asked her, "Do you mind if I join you?"

"No, I do not mind," she said. They made small talk. Finally, it was time for her to get back to her work area. As she walked toward the elevator, she noticed a shadow behind her. Once she entered, he came in as well.

As she began to push the button, he moved his hand toward hers and stopped the elevator. He looked into her eyes. "Don't be frightened," he said.

She said, "I am not afraid at all."

Stephen asked Monica if she was married, and she said no. Then, he admitted to being married, but he confessed to being so unhappy. He told her that he and his wife had been married for more than twenty years. He said that he was no longer attracted to his wife. Stephen said that he slept in the guest bedroom because his wife snored all night, and he had a hard time sleeping. So, they barely made love. Because they had a home together, it was difficult to leave because she would take him to court, and she most likely would win because of her medical condition. So, Monica said, "Why don't you get a divorce and start over?" He told her that his two sons were not local, and they asked him to hang in there until she could go live with one of them. Well, you can figure out what happened. They started dating.

Stephen took Monica to a restaurant in Maryland. They had a nice rib dinner after they ate she agreed to go to her place. They became sexually involved. He called her every day for six months. Took walks in the park. Once he even took her out to a hotel and promised to spend the night. However, once they had sex, he decided that it would be best to go home to keep things from looking suspicious. The next day, Stephen did not call. She was worried because this had never happened before. Then, she went by his job, and he was too busy to make time for her.

She waited in her car in the parking lot for five hours until he got off. Once he came out, she asked him to get in her Mercedes, and she demanded an explanation. He told her that he decided to end the relationship because he felt guilty about what had transpired between them. She was shocked. Tears streamed down her face. Then she told him that she was two months pregnant. He reached for her hand, and he squeezed it. "Monica," he said, "I do not want a baby with you. I love my wife."

She started the ignition and put the car in drive. She locked the doors and proceeded to have a head-on collision with a trash truck. Her plan was to kill them both. Suddenly, a young child ran into the street, and she stopped the car. That saved both their lives. She released the lock and told him to get out. She got an abortion and went into counseling.

Three years later, she committed suicide because she got involved with another married man. He left her as well. Woman, pay attention to the red flags. The minute that he indicates there is a wife involved, tell him good-bye. Step aside and keep on walking to the nearest exit. Do not be betrayed by a man's lies. If he is so unhappy, then why is his wife's picture in his wallet or on his desk at the office? Let your guard down when the time is right, and keep your drawers up.

Karen was married for over fifteen years. She never bore children. She worked during the day, and her husband worked in the evening. On several occasions, she traveled to Spain because she was a buyer for Lord and Taylor. Upon her return, she was eager to get home from the airport to have sex with her husband. Andre was a passionate and romantic lover.

When he touched Karen, it sent chills down her spine. But suddenly, he made excuses not to have sex. His biggest complaint was back pain. However, he found strength to go bowling with the fellows on the weekend. Three months passed, and they still had not had sex. Karen returned home from a business trip at about midnight. As she walked into the house, she noticed a red light on in the dining room area. She took of her coat. As she launched forward, she identified two images on the table moving up and down.

She saw a woman on top of her husband. They were so engrossed in having sex that they did not even hear her come in the house. She let them continue. Then she walked upstairs and called the police. She reported that her husband was in the house having sex with another woman, and she was about to kill them both. The police tried to deter her, but she was not listening. She loaded the shotgun that was hidden in the closet in the spare bedroom. Karen put on a pair of blue sweatpants, a black top, and tennis shoes. She put her hair in a ponytail, and she put on black gloves. After easing back downstairs, she found them lying there still naked. She switched on the light. As she pointed the gun at them, she told Andre to get off the table and hold his penis outward.

He was shaking like it was zero degrees in the house. Then she took the gun and shot his penis of. The woman was in shock. Karen shot her twice in the stomach. She greeted the police ten minutes later. The woman was her boss. She never paid attention to the red flags. Her boss used to visit unexpectedly. She started eating dinner with them on Sundays, and there were times when she spent the night after they finished working on an intense project.

Rita was married at the age of twenty-four years old. Skip was extremely attentive, and he bought her everything that her heart desired. They had two children, and he was the primary provider. He cooked all the meals. He paid a babysitter to watch the children when they went out to the movies. After a long day at work, Rita asked the babysitter if she would come over to sit with the kids until her husband came home because she wanted to take a nap.

When she arrived, she showed up with her cousin, who was Rita's co-worker. After sleeping for five hours, Rita woke up and came downstairs. She smelled the fried chicken, greens, and macaroni and cheese. Rita was so pleased. When she entered the kitchen, she saw a lady who was unfamiliar standing at the stove. Then her husband came home, and the babysitter decided to take the kids to the park for a few hours. Rita kissed Skip on the cheek and left to pick up her mom.

After passing five blocks, she got a flat tire. She turned around, came back home, and called her husband from the cell phone. He did not answer. She walked into the family room, and no one was there. She headed toward the bedroom on the first floor. The fire was burning in the fire place.

She saw Skip and Coressa having sex in the guest room. Rita was devastated. She picked up the poker from the fireplace, heated it, and jammed it into Skip's right eye. Come on, women, you may have single female friends, but don't let them cook in your kitchen without your consent. Rita ignored the red flag.

Continue with Your Own Happiness

It is imperative to stay on track in your life. We all must learn to drop our pride at some point. Never worry about how stupid you may feel in the eyes of others. There isn't one of us who has not been played a fool. Paying attention to the red flags will save you from heartache in the long run. People who wear a mask have a hidden agenda. They never admit to you what their true intentions are in the beginning of the relationship.

We need to let God be our messenger .He sends a message to us. However, it is up to each of us to pay attention and receive the message. When your spouse comes home early every day with alcohol on his breath, pay attention to the red flags. He may have become an alcoholic. It is imperative to stay inspired by positive changes in your life. Hold onto those things that bring out the best in you. Never regress back to your old ways. There is no room for feeling guilty about past mistakes.

Moving forward is all that is necessary to improve your way of living. There are red flags at the end of the road, and it is for the good of all men and women to pay attention before the bomb is dropped and there is no way to turn back. Each day, I look through my open window, and I take a deep breath to feel the fresh air and to allow my soul to open up to the earth. Women, never forget how important your feelings are to you. Your emotions tell the truth about how you are *Flags* feeling in general. Hold onto the light, and never spend time in the dark with no apparent reason. Someday your prince charming will come to push those doubts out of your mind. Never in life are we to be abused and used by anyone.

Each of us has a desire to be loved and provided for to some extent. Not knowing what is happening in a relationship causes one to lose a lot of sleep, miss work, drink, or use drugs. Paying attention to the red flags will stop the emergency room visits in the middle of the night. Therefore, in the midst of it all, we must show up in order to provide a sense of peace for ourselves.

Women, if he is calling you names, pay attention. That is verbal abuse. When he stops saying thanks for dinner, pay attention; he is thanking someone else. If he is not concerned that you are upset, pay attention; he is not in love with you anymore. Some men like to argue for no reason. At times, they want the woman to be miserable. Do not waste time on foolish behavior.

Pack your bags, and leave the man in the dust. Stop trying to make an excuse for what he is doing that makes you so unhappy. For the time being, he is the one who is causing the problem. Not once will he admit that he needs to receive some form of therapy.

Paying attention to the red flags will save you from years

of heartache and pain. Never let your past dictate what you can and cannot do with your life. A positive attitude is the starting point of deciding what you will accomplish. After years of being told that there is no need in striving toward your dreams, you begin to believe that it is impossible to become that attorney, musician, dancer, doctor, social worker, judge, professional entertainer, or millionaire. No one can see into your future but God.

Some people tend to be intimidated of those who have the desire and guts to be who God created them to be. Fret not thyself because of evil men neither be thou envious at the wicked (Proverbs 24:19). Each day, take time to meditate on the goodness of God, and he will lead you in the right direction. When those negative red flags pop up, leave them up so that they catch your attention. These flags are relevant issues that you need to take action on to find peace within your soul. For example, when a man is verbally abusive and then later he turns into prince charming, be aware: he is a control freak. His goal is to make you feel bad about yourself.

Ladies, when you make excuses for him, you encourage him to continue mistreating you. Remember; never be a doormat for anyone. Here is a case of a man fulfilling his dreams. I met Gregory on December 5, 2007. His mother was dying from cancer. He needed someone to talk to, so he told me his life story. Years ago, Gregory was a graduate student at Tennessee University working on a degree in education.

While in the study hall, he met a tall and attractive African American female. They hit it off right away. They started eating lunch together, and they both decided to date. After being together for about a year, he asked her where she saw them in the future. Her response to him was "I do not see us anywhere because you do not make enough money."

His heart was broken. However, he had a desire to have a wife and create a beautiful family. Therefore, he picked his ego up of the floor, and he let nature take its course. Finally, he met a woman who was pursing her master's degree in education. She was of medium built with long blonde hair and blue eyes. Melissa was Caucasian. She had a smile to die for. While in the school cafeteria, she noticed him sitting alone, and she asked him if she could join him. He agreed to allow her into his space. As time passed, they would meet for dinner after their last class in the evening. They were acquaintances, friends, and then lovers. Three years passed, and he asked her to marry him.

However, there was a stipulation. He said, "I need you to promise me that we can have two children together." She agreed, and they got married three months later. They now have two beautiful girls, eight and twelve years old. Melissa and Gregory both completed their education, and they received

Ph.D.'s. They are now college professors in Denver, Colorado. He has received several awards for his outstanding performance, which has allowed him to receive a handsome salary. Now he is an entrepreneur, and he has a multimillion- dollar business. If the first woman had been patient and kind, she would have gotten the money from him that she felt was important. Later, she came back to tell him that she had made a mistake. However, it was too late. He looked into her eyes and told her, "Love does not live here anymore." Because she was not paying attention, she lost a precious jewel. This is just an example that there are some good men in the world.

Four Rules to Dating

Dating can be a lot of fun. Never have sex unless you absolutely want to. Don't allow a man to pressure you into being intimate when you have no desire for him. If he is interested in you, he will be patient and respectful towards you. Sleeping with a stranger is not an appropriate behavior on a first date. Take your time. If he insists on having sex, pay attention to the red flags because he is most likely looking for a one-night stand. You can flip a coin. Heads, you say no. Tails, you leave. Each woman he has slept with will be sleeping with you as well.

Therefore, use protection to prevent pregnancy and diseases. A man should be polite, come to the door, and knock when he takes you out on a date. Never respond to a man blowing his horn for you to come out for a date. It is nice to have someone provide for you. However, never depend on a man to provide 100 percent of your living expenses, not even your own husband. Remember, your boyfriend, husband, or lover may go away, but bills last a lifetime.

Guilty by Association

Each of us have people with whom we associate who are not on our level. Some drink, smoke, and use drugs. Although you may not have some of these habits, you are guilty by association. If you notice a man cannot deal with you unless he has his bottle of wine, be aware: he most likely does not want to be in your presence when he is sober. Bad habits rub of onto us, and before we know it, we are acting different. Trust your gut feelings.

Pay close attention to the words that he uses, and do not allow him to disrespect you anymore. No one really wants to deal with an incompetent man When you choose the wrong person, stop blaming your friends and family members for the decisions that you have made. Each of us was given a brain, and you must learn from your mistakes by not repeating them. It is imperative that we bury the past. Pack that entire box and bury it in the backyard or burn it in the furnace. There will come a time when you must let your guards down in order to meet a decent and caring individual. Holding back your feelings will scare a man away. Just relax, take deep breaths, and let go and let God.

After being hurt so many times, we develop a sense of pride. Drop that pride in order to attract a winner. Having too much pride can destroy a relationship. So keep moving forward, and stop hiding from the world. You are too beautiful to be alone. Your heart is pure, and you are one of God's favorite angels. Never forget the time when you were so confident in yourself. There is no room for being ashamed of what has taken place a year ago or yesterday. Today is a new day.

Women, you are reading this book because you realize that you are so amazing, full of life, love, peace, and happiness. So breathe in some fresh air, let it happen, and you will capture the truth when a person opens his mouth for the first time. It is time to find your own way. Stop depending on your family and friends to find your mate. You can do it yourself. Just trust that you have what it takes to have a healthy, safe, and loving relationship.

Once you do this, you will for sure be able to find your own way. Step out, and meet new people. Do not be afraid of rejection. If a man turns you down, count it as a blessing to meet someone else. It is his loss and another man's gain. Stop living like a caged woman. Come out of the house. If you are not satisfied with your looks, do something about it. Exercise daily, cut back on sweets, drink plenty of water, and eat a healthy meal each day. No matter how you look, it is important to be proud of who you are at this moment.

Ladies, do not lose weight for him; do it for yourself. It is time to set yourself free from all the negative thoughts. Let love find you, and write yourself letters. Tell yourself how important you are to all mankind. Bury the dead, and then you will be ready to make the change. You will find that you have less stress, and you will be able to roll with the punches.

Remember, never quit no matter what comes your way. Your self-confidence will increase, and you will be able to face any obstacle that appears. Stop living in denial, and shift your focus to more positive thoughts. There is a solution to any situation that you must face. The message is clear to you right now. You must have the will power to stay away from men who mistreat you. Women, just say no, walk away, and never look back. Your individuality should strengthen your love.

You have what is required to meet the needs of yourself and others. I have had the pleasure of meeting the greatest female legends of all time. As for myself, I strive not to let other women down by settling for less. In life, we all have been let down by those we love. However, you are the real deal and a true class act. As you continue to serve God, he will ensure that everything works out for the better.

You must watch how you treat people because you are made in the image of God. Whatever you do to others, you do to God. Women, when you stay pitiful, sad, and broken, you give your power away to those who have hurt you. Blaming others is a waste of time. In life, we make choices. With every choice, there are consequences, whether they are good or bad.

Hillary was in her late twenties when she met Dusty. They attended the same college. They both were studying to become lawyers. The first day that they met, there was a physical attraction. One day after class, he asked her if they could talk. He reached for her hand, and the adrenaline began to flow. Her heart skipped a beat, and he was sweating. Come to find out, he was married with two kids. One child was from his marriage, and one was from a past relationship.

Hillary and Dusty went to dinner. There was an instant connection. After spending a long afternoon in the park together, they agreed that the relationship was meant to be. He promised never to have sex with his wife anymore. He said, "I stay with her because I do not want to leave my daughter." According to Hillary, he felt that she was too young to understand if he left.

Every day after work, he went to Hillary's house, and they made passionate love. He was very compassionate, loving, gentle, giving, and thoughtful. They went to the gym, and he took her to dinner on several occasions. Hillary had his home number and his address. She called him at work and home. She knew some of his co-workers and friends. He promised Hillary that they would be together someday later in the future. Dusty's wife was a registered nurse, and she worked long hours. Hillary used to go to his daughter's school programs, and she attended his son's graduation. Each day, they took a shower together, and he rocked her world. Dusty was living a double life, and his wife was not paying attention to the red flags. This relationship lasted for three years. One morning, Hillary received a phone call from Dusty, and he told her that he wanted to come by and cook dinner for her.

After they ate, he dropped the bomb. He told Hillary that he and his wife were drinking a bottle of wine one night, and they both had the desire to have sex. Hillary was devastated, and she never looked at men quite the same. She could not understand how the relationship could have ended this way. Hillary was not paying any attention to the red flags. The minute he told her that he was married, she should have said to him, "No thanks, I do not date married men."

Three months passed. Hillary woke up one morning with a headache and vomiting. She called her doctor, and he told her to come into his office the same day. Once she arrived, the vomiting got worse. The doctor ran blood tests, and it was determined that Hillary was three months pregnant. She began to cry. The doctor offered to call the baby's father, and she declined.

Hillary was all alone. Her friends were not supportive, and they disrespected her for dating a married man. Then she broke down and called Dusty. They met the next morning at her home. He was in a rage when she told him about the baby. He could not believe that she was trying to ruin his life. Hillary was completely lost. Dusty insisted that she get an abortion. He did not want his wife to find out about their relationship. He was not the same man that she met three years ago. He had changed. Anyway, Hillary mustered up the strength, and she told him that he was crazy. She was determined to have the baby. It did not matter whether he would be involved in their lives. As he continued to exhibit his nasty attitude, Hillary's thoughts were flowing like the wind in the night. She was a mild-spoken person, polite, hardworking, and loyal to those she cared about.

Dusty pushed the wrong button when he told her that his wife was pregnant as well. Tears began to stream down her face. She gave him a smile, and she asked him to leave. He said, "Don't you get it? I am never going to marry you, Hillary. I love my wife."

She took a deep breath, and she said, "I am really happy for you, Dusty. Close the door on your way out."

After about twenty-three years, Dusty and his wife moved to West Virginia to be closer to their son. His law firm was doing exceptionally well. One of his employees, Shirley, was suing him for sexual harassment. Dusty offered to take Shirley out for dinner one evening. Then they went to her home to have sex.

He was being recorded. Another day, he wrote on a

napkin that he wanted to have oral sex and Shirley kept the napkin. Finally, he took her to California for a business conference that consisted of over 400 people. She was one of the presenters. Shirley introduced herself to the audience and requested that the projector be pulled down and the lights get a little dim. She said, "I would like to take this time to conduct this presentation with the help of one of the most uncaring, thoughtless, heartbreaking, and unfaithful men in this world."

The audience could not believe what she said. Then Shirley began to show the slides of them having sex, and each packet contained a picture of them having sex in his office on the desk. Little did he know, to add insult to injury, Shirley was his wife's sister. The sisters were not close, and they had not seen each other in over ten years. Shirley had never met Dusty before.

To be honest, Shirley did not even know that her sister was married. Shirley contacted a reputable law firm in Washington DC that was owned by Hillary and her associates. Shirley sued Dusty for two million dollars, his wife left him, and Hillary came forward and told the wife about their affair.

Dusty was arrested for back payment for child support. The two women opened their own mentoring program to help other women to avoid getting involved with married men. Women, beware of those men who strive to deceive you by masquerading as a single man (for example, he only meets you at a restaurant, calls only at a certain time of the day, is never available at night, indicates that he is separated, and only has time for you on the weekends).

Hillary is now married to a terrific man. He is a man of his word. Her son by Dusty is doing great. He went to medical school, and he is now a doctor.

Caroline was married. However, she got divorced after two years. She did not have any children. Each day, she would come home from work and spend time sitting on her porch. She lived in a small town where everyone knew each other. Harold was married. They were actually next-door neighbors. His wife was in school to become a nurse practitioner. Getting her rest was so important.

He became bored, so he used Caroline as a sounding board. After meeting with him daily, they got really close. At night, they spent time talking about how his wife was not meeting his needs. Then Harold's wife got pregnant. He pretended to be disappointed because he said that he could not afford to have any children. Being pregnant and going to school was taking its toll on Harold's wife, and she lost her interest in sex. So he said.

About six months later, Caroline allowed Harold to sneak into her house after hours. They had sex twice a week. Then, one night, they went to a tourist home in Washington DC, and

Caroline's brother was there with one of his girlfriends.

He noticed Harold with Caroline. Harold's brother-in-law punched him in the face, and they started fighting. They were both arrested. Finally, Harold's wife picked him up from jail. She was surprised to find out that Harold had been having sex with Caroline. They made up, and Harold ended the relationship with Caroline. Two months later, Caroline tried to commit suicide.

Currently, she is in a mental institution and being closely monitored by a psychiatrist. Pay attention to the red flags. Men who cheat always talk badly about their spouse. For some odd reason, they know exactly how to play on women's feelings. Caroline lived next door. She knew that they were living together. There was no way she could see what was happening behind closed doors.

She was only listening to Harold's lies. Having faith in God is the most rewarding thing in this life. He is the only one that you should be sharing in a marriage. Women tend to feel worthless if they are not married, involved in a relationship, or have a man to love them. One must love herself before being able to be in a healthy loving relationship. Women tend to attract men who they do not want. Subconsciously, women are seeking to have these types of relationships. These women suffer from low self-esteem which causes them to have high anxiety levels. They are unable to find a healthy loving relationship. These women do not have the ability to think in a positive manner.

At times, they lose control, and they blame others for their mistakes. This is not to say that all women have problems in this area. The fact that you are reading this book tells me that you have been in one or more of these situations. Help is always available. It starts with just saying no to married men.

Every woman can lead another woman in the right direction. You are beautiful, strong willed, lovable, and able to have a fulfilling relationship with a man who is available. Not all men cheat. There is a man waiting patiently for you to get over that liar that you are dating. Don't be blindsided. Trust yourself to make healthy choices. Ask God to help you make intelligent decisions in order to prevent you from ruining your life. Living in fear will hold you back. There is no other like you. Each day, look into the mirror.

Tell yourself that you are beautiful. Nurture and pamper yourself. Making a major impact in others' lives is the key to being successful in life. As you travel this road, never feel like you are alone. I am here to support your dreams. Keep monitoring your attitude, keep records of your dates, and throw away the bad seeds. When you get hurt, it is important to recognize that the pain does exist because holding onto dead weight will only pull you down. Having guilty feelings of being responsible for bad circumstances that have happened to you must stop. Women, you are human, and you all make mistakes.

Just be sure to learn from them, and strive to never repeat them. Men will make you believe they will suffer greatly if you do not respond positively to their requests, and they will call on your guilt to respond to their requests, even when it means violating your rights. Men will accuse you of misdeeds, words, or actions to arouse your sense of guilt and make you believe you are the one with a problem in an interpersonal relationship difficulty because this takes the pressure off of men this manipulation uses your guilt to benefit them.

Depression

I have had many women who suffer from depression come into my office. For the most part, they can't figure out why they are feeling like this. They say they have a good life and a solid relationship. However, as they talk, they realize that many things are missing in their love life, things they don't want to look at. Why? Because they fear that if they face the truth, ultimately they might end up alone. Women think they are better of not knowing. But in order to break the cycle of depression, one must be honest. As one patient told me, "truth is my friend; it will guide me in a good direction." One man said that he could not figure out why he felt depressed.

Marylou was a forty-nine-year-old single African American female movie producer, who reported to the hospital emergency room with complaints of depression and the thought of driving her van of a bridge. Marylou was attractive, tall, and dark-haired, and she was wearing glasses. Marylou appeared to be in considerable distress, and she had a lack of energy. Marylou reported a six-month period of increasingly persistent dysphoria, which is a lack of energy and feeling as if she were made of lead. Marylou had recently been spending seventeen to twenty-two hours a day in her bed because she did not want to interact with other people. Marylou reported daily episodes of binge eating during the day and night. She would consume thirteen large boxes of chocolate chip cookies at one time. Marylou reported problems with intermittent binge eating since adolescence, but these episodes had recently increased in frequency, resulting in a twenty pound weight gain over the last few months. In the past, Marylou's weight had often fluctuated greatly as she went on and of a variety of diets.

Marylou denied preoccupation with thinness, a history of episodes of vomiting, and other weight-reduction procedures to compensate for the binge eating. She attributed her increasing symptoms to marriage difficulties that led to divorce after being married for twenty-five years. Her marriage fell apart the night she came home from work and found her husband in their bed with her two sisters having sex. Years ago, she suspected that something was going on, but she kept pushing down those red flags.

Marylou was fired from her job four weeks before going to the emergency room. She claimed that she owed her mortgage company $30,000. Then Marylou admitted to stealing $42,000 from her place of employment. For six months, she used her employer's credit card to buy new clothes. Marylou denied past or present symptoms of mania, obsessive thoughts, or a compulsion to buy. She reported that spending money alleviated her chronic feelings of loneliness, isolation, and sadness.

Experiencing only temporary relief every day of her life, Marylou would impulsively buy expensive jewelry, watches, or multiple pairs of the same shoes. Two years ago, her employers noticed the massive credit card bills.

Marylou had nothing she could sell to reduce the debt. Her employers allowed her to pay of the debts by continuing to work for them and giving them part of her salary, but she could not stop her spending. Marylou would open a checking account at one bank and then overdraw from that account to open a second account at another bank. Over two years, this escalating process led to her additional $300,000 debt.

Two weeks after Marylou's fraudulent acts, she was arrested. The news made the front page of *The Washington Post*. Therefore, her employers discovered the arrest, and Marylou was promptly dismissed from her place of employment, which led to her current desperate state. In addition, Marylou had lifelong memories of beatings and verbal assaults from her husband. She had recurrent thoughts of death (not just a fear of dying), recurrent suicidal ideation without a specific plan, and a suicide attempt. Marylou had insomnia or hypersomnia nearly every day. She was admitted to the hospital for inpatient management of depression, and she hung herself two days later.

At times, each of us get stressed out or feels tied from time to time. For some, this feeling may last for months or years. A large number of people with depression do not get treatment, and they don't realize that depression is an illness that will not go away without proper treatment.

Marylou entered the hospital when she could see no way out of her elevating personal difficulties. Marylou had a major depressive episode, with symptoms of depressed mood, overeating, overspending, sleeping over twelve hours a day, and a loss of energy and interest. Marylou's marriage problems were the result of an inability to resist what Marylou called spending binges that somehow decreased her feelings of emptiness and sadness.

Marylou said that she felt sad and worthless. Almost all depressed people complain about reduced energy, difficulty finishing assignments, feeling impaired at work, and they have no motivation to take on new projects.

If they do, they usually do not complete
them.

Those Who Suffer from Depression May Need Treatment

People who suffer from chronic depression need to be treated. At times, they can see a therapist on a short-term basis, but longer-term therapy may be needed to prevent recurrences. No one paid attention to the red flags. Alice is a single white female. She reported to her family sad feelings and not being able to provide for herself. There was never any suggestion for her to seek help. Individual therapy would have helped Alice to increase her ability to care for her own needs and decrease the frequency and intensity of her repetitive thoughts.

Psychotherapy treatment would have helped Alice gain control of her behavior in order to move on with her life in a more positive way. Certainly, it would have helped her thought process. Some antidepressant medications would have decreased Alice's depression. Attending group therapy would have provided support, and it would have helped Alice to interact with other people with the same issue.

Depression Questionnaire

1. Are you feeling slowed down or tired and unable to sit still for long periods?
2. Are you feeling guilty or worthless?
3. Are you having problems concentrating, thinking, or making decisions?
4. Are you having sex problems?
5. Are you worried or suffering from anxiety?
6. Are you having thoughts of suicide?
7. Do you have headaches often?
8. Do you have digestive problems?
9. Do you find yourself sleeping long hours?

After taking this quiz, if you have more than five symptoms, talk to a friend, family member, or professional to seek help.

What Can Guilt Do to You?

Guilt can make you too focus on striving to make life perfect. You overwork. You tend to over give of yourself. You are willing to do anything in your attempt to make everyone happy. You are over conscientious. Your fretting will not change the past. This is your life. No one can live it for you. Although you may not have responded quickly by leaving a bad situation in the past, give yourself accolades for having the guts to leave now.

Feelings of guilt for putting up with his crap for so long, for not speaking up when he disrespected you in front of your friends, cannot help him to become a better man. His misfortune is not your problem. You have a sense of right and wrong. His wrong doing inhibited him from treating you like a woman. It is imperative to not let others play on your feelings of guilt. Maybe you believe the man will suffer greatly if you do not respond positively to his requests. As you know, most abusers will threaten with negative consequences, like going to jail or to the hospital or divorcing you. This manipulation uses your guilt to benefit them.

Secrets Men Hide on the Inside

If you notice that he enjoys spending more time with his male friends than with you, pay attention. Most likely there is something going on when is he out. Women, no man who is in love with a woman wants to hang with other men most of the time instead of being at home with his wife or girlfriend. He could be on the down low. I interviewed several men who told me that married men pick them up in the clubs. These men have children and have been married for years.

One man said that he had a brother who is married, and he has been having sex with men for many years. Another young man said that he sleeps with women and men, and his girlfriend does not have a clue. Women, I know this is a touchy question to ask a man; however, it is imperative that you know the truth to protect yourselves from catching diseases. A man on the down low believes in his heart that he is not gay. Then why is it a secret? If men are not ashamed of their behavior, then they need to be open about it. It is not normal to see two men drinking out of each other's wine glasses. Pay attention to the red flags.

They are sharing more than just wine. Men on the down low are fearful of being exposed to the world because they do not want to be stereotyped. They need to take the women's feelings and rights into consideration. Women have a right to know who their man is sexually active with. It is not fair to leave women in the dark. Remember, some men may never come out of the closet. You must pay attention to the red flags in order to spare yourself of a life filled with lies and deceit. When a man is lying, he tends to use less hand movements, his expression is likely stiff, and he might touch his chin or scratch his nose. When a man is being dishonest, his eyes move a lot in order to avoid meeting up with your gaze. Furthermore, if he looks at your eyes for a long period of time that is a sure sign that he is lying.

Listen Without Interrupting Your Man

When he speaks, listen with an open mind. There is no room to read his mind. If there is something that does not make sense to you, ask him to explain. A real man will have no problem communicating with you. Lack of understanding of each other may destroy thc relationship. If you stay together, your listening skills will improve.

Be Loyal to Yourself

Women have compromised their happiness for the sake of men for years. It is time to overcome the fear of being alone. Women, let him know exactly how you are feeling. This will save you from a lot of heartache and pain. You will find that some men are not concerned with making you happy when they are dealing with their own personal issues. For example, not getting along with his boss, if he is having problems on his job, he needs to deal with them appropriately.

If a man truly loves you, he will not want the job to interfere with his relationship with you. Women tend to nurture men, and you hurt when they hurt. Most women strive to assist in making life better for men. However, they need to recognize when it is time to move on in order to accomplish their goals. Women, it is important to be supportive. However, let the men find their way. Don't look for a job for them, don't call out sick for them, and don't lose sleep because they are too lazy to look for employment elsewhere.

One man who I used to talk to complained about his boss every day. My advice to him was to have a conversation with his boss or simply look for employment elsewhere. Instead, he was so stuck in this black/white mentality that he felt it was only white folks who treated black men badly. After educating him that he was blaming others for his failure, the friendship ended because I was not about to waste another day on a hopeless case. Can some of you identify with me?

Blaming others for their own unhappiness only turns women of. No one wants a relationship with a man who thinks little of himself. Remember, if he thinks little of himself he can't think too much of you. When you end one relationship, make good choices. Don't fall back into the hands of the devil. He knows your desires to be loved. He will send another married man who will complain about his wife, and he'll make you believe that you are the one for him. He will blackball her.

Don't be fooled by his lies. Ask yourself these questions: If he is so unhappy, why is he still living there? Why does he go home every night? A man who is unhappy at home will leave way before you walk into his life. Most men have a plan, and they know who to pick and where to look for a desperate woman. Women who are on the prowl can be spotted a long way off. Pay attention to the red flags.

A married man has nothing to offer you, women, but heartache and pain. You deserve your own healthy relationship. Nothing saddens me more than to see a woman dating that same man for over five years only to find out he has been with someone other than her. Don't be fooled by the roses and late-night dinners. Treat yourself well. Never settle for crumbs. No one can save you but yourself. Keep positive thoughts flowing. Women tend to believe that there is only one person for them. Too often attraction is mistaken for rightness. A sign of an abusive person can often be found after several dates if you pay attention to the red flags. Women, ask questions and do some investigating into his history. In most abusive relationships, the man tries to control you by withholding sex.

An emotionally abusive man is harder to identify, and an experience abusive man can make you think you are not good enough for him. It is just as difficult to recover from emotional abuse as it is from physical abuse. Emotional abuse causes low self-esteem, bipolar disorder, or depression. An abusive man may tell you he loves you. "That is why I beat you," he may say. "I will change." So you won't leave or divorce him.

The more times you take him back, the more control he will gain over you. Make sure you pay attention to the red flags. We tend to give away our oxygen even when we cannot breathe, not realizing that we are suffocating. If we get sick, we will not be able to take care of the children, work, or be a wife to a good man later in life. If he is beating you, get out of the relationship. Save your money, go to a shelter, call your family, and ask them to let you move in for a while. Leave when he is not home. Do not provoke him.

Negativity

Negativity is contagious. It is like a terminal disease. We walk around like normal but we are being eaten up inside. Change is gradual, and there are different strategies that are effective. Here are a few: positive self-talk, professional help, and self-confidence.

These strategies will help us to learn how to help ourselves so that we no longer allow fear to be an obstacle to our happiness and reaching some of our own personal goals. There is no reason for anyone to think of themselves as a failure. Your future success or failure is in your hands.

Take Yourself Off the Market

Take yourself of the market. We promote our bodies like they are on sale. We advertise by exposing most of our cleavage and wearing very short shorts to show of our butt. Be aware, men like to use their imagination. Showing too much, it's a turnoff. Learn how to communicate by having a conversation with each other. Stop communicating with your precious body. You are not a product.

You are a beautiful human being. Save the promoting and advertising for when you start your own company. We are not a man's customer. Therefore, avoid encouraging them to buy your body. A relationship is based on learning about each other and striving to find areas where you both are compatible. This leads to a healthy and lasting relationship. Women who have a need to advertise are seeking self-gratification and excitement, which does not lead to a lasting relationship.

These types of behaviors reflect one's self-esteem, and the relationship has no value, which is neither normal nor healthy. A healthy relationship consists of less stress, and it's full of happiness. It's imperative that you are aware of what constitutes a healthy relationship.

Promiscuity with Different Men All Over Again

Being sexually active with different men can lead to the spread of AIDS. It is a disease that cannot wash of. This type of disease can become widespread and become a societal issue that leads to mental illnesses or drug addiction due to depression after being diagnosed with having the disease. As we know, there are times when your husband, lover, or stranger may decide to rape you.

It is a woman's worst nightmare. Some women never report that they have been raped by their husband or significant other. Although some women contact the crisis center and receive counseling, when it comes time to prosecute the criminal, they tend to change their mind. I have sat in on several cases in court where the wife or girlfriend has told the prosecutor that she does not want to press charges, and the man was set free. There is a myth that women bring rape on themselves by the way they dress. I don't believe that any woman should be violated.

Pay attention to the red flags. A date rapist may appear to be strong and in charge of everything, try to impress other males around him, and may show hostility toward most women. Believe it or not, a rapist can be a very handsome man, and he will pick women who are insecure about themselves.

Take Your Time

Healthy relationships are built on a solid foundation. If you are experiencing a divorce or recent breakup from a long-lasting relationship, or if you've moved out after shacking up for years, it takes time to move on with a new relationship. When you rush into another relationship, it is built on shaky ground. Loneliness leads to unpleasant outcomes. When the relationship is built on a solid foundation, it is considered fixed or firm.

When the relationship is unstable, it wavers and lacks steadiness. There is no emotional control. It is difficult to eliminate stress in this type of relationship. Too much stress may disrupt one's emotional state of mind. Women are emotional creatures. We blame stress on our spouse, friends, family, or whomever we are upset with instead of accepting responsibility. It is not what people do to us that upsets us; it is our response to what a person does to us. Know that you are one of the most special women in the world. Disappointments will come. Don't let them take control over you. Tell yourself that you will make it through. Love yourself. Talk to those who support you.

The normal relationship consists of praise and support from your mate. If he calls you names, if he curses at you and later makes as though nothing happened, don't be surprised if he is suffering from a mental illness. Healthy behavior lacks verbal abuse. Women, pay attention to the red flags. Everything that dresses nice, smells good, and looks gorgeous may not be normal.

The devil dresses up in suits, and he will attack at any time. Stop making excuses as to why you must stay with this nonparticipant and unstable man. The situation will never get better until he recognizes that he has a problem and seeks help. Loving him more will not lead to him loving you or himself. The real point is that you can do bad by yourself.

How to Avoid Becoming Too Emotionally Involved

Marjorie agreed to go on a date with Will. After the third date, friction developed. Will suggested that Marjorie date other men. Marjorie was not interested in anyone else, and she tried to compromise, particularly because she felt rejected by him. After considerable effort, Marjorie asked Will out on another date. Will realized that Marjorie was becoming overly involved. A week later, he asked her to stop calling him. Marjorie felt unloved.

When women become too emotionally involved with men, they have a reduced capacity to help themselves. There are several types of irrational thinking that lead to over involvement. It seems that emotional involvement with a man is unavoidable. It is healthy to become emotionally involved to some degree because it creates an environment where the man and woman are comfortable expressing their feelings to each other. However, how do women strike a balance between not caring and caring too much where it makes them sick and unable to function? The way to have balance is to do things that you like. For example, exercise, and spend time with friends and family. These things give you strong positive energy. Women who have been taught personal self-care has balance in their lives. They understand the importance of saying no when they feel uncomfortable with saying yes to a man. Pulling away from the emotional issues will help keep balance in your life. Make sure that you find time for yourself so that you will not lose sight of who you are.

Positive Thinker

The power of positive thinking is the best gift that God has given to us. Your belief in things going right will help you to attract the finest things in life. Whatever conditions you are facing at this time are the results of your thinking. The situation will change, but you have to change your thinking first. Positive thinking is the first step in getting you up and moving toward your goals. It will give you a bright outlook on your future, and thinking positive leads to pleasant emotions.

Do not let anyone make you feel negative. It can suck the life out of you. Be aware of your thoughts and conversations with people. Understand this, if everyone is talking negatively around you, you will eventually start talking negatively as well. So pick up, and walk out of the room when it is appropriate. Stay as focused as possible. Trust me, your friends, colleagues, husband, and family members are watching and listening to what you are saying.

Although you may have some negative thoughts in your mind, ask God to remove them. As I interact with people, I encourage them to stay positive, and it helps me to stay focused and positive because when I say it to others, I am pointing the finger at me first. Some feel that life is not fair. God is fair, and he will take great care of you. Remember what you are worth. Trust God for all your needs. Forever believe in yourself. Hold your head high. I am here with you. Trust yourself to make good decisions.

Men have their own issues. Breaking up could be the best thing for both of you. One man told me that he was having some health issues. Those problems affected his sex life. It took a sex therapist and a physician to point out that his low sex drive was caused by him having unprotected sex with so many different women. Remain hopeful because you are one in a million.

When a man makes a mistake, he should be willing to admit to it and tell you that he is sorry for hurting you. But some men are afraid to open up and admit that they are wrong. Men do not recognize a good woman until she has walked out of their life. Just remember, when a man truly loves you, he will not let his personal problems get in the way of a healthy relationship. He will communicate well with you, and he will not keep you guessing.

Moving On After a Breakup

Once the relationship has ended, there should not be any contact between you and your ex. Block his number from your home and cell phone. Get rid of the jewelry that he bought for you or return it via mail. Keeping in contact with your ex leads to heartache and pain. If kids are involved, deal with your ex in relation to the kids only. For example, if he starts talking about the past, interrupt him, and remind him why the conversation is taking place.

Do not allow him to take you into precarious waters. Strive to remain at peace. If you engage in an abusive argument with your ex while talking to him on the phone, take a hard look in the mirror because you are getting something out of being abused. Allow yourself enough time to heal. Do not join the dating game right away because you will get infatuation and love mixed up. Too often, women jump into another relationship too fast. Slow down, and get to know the man before telling him about your ex. spending quality time together is healthy, but do not have sex right away. He may not be the one who you are looking to spend years with, and you may not be the one for him. Good men do not like to be rushed. Get past your past issues first, and you will be able to create a healthy relationship with someone new.

Bad-mouthing the Parent

When relationships end, the ex-spouse or ex-girlfriend tends to bad-mouth the man. Women, the children have nothing to do with your breakup. Do not ruin the relationship between the child and his or her father. If you handle the situation inappropriately, the children will grow up and turn on you. Keep the children out of the drama.

They should not get tangled up in the mess. The children should be allowed to spend time with their dad unless there is some form of abuse problem. Make every effort to maintain a trustworthy relationship with your children. You have been a terrific mom. Keep it that way. Pay attention to the red flags. Your children will start showing signs of resentment by acting out and doing poorly in school if they are upset with you for not letting them see their father.

Pitfalls for Women

Some women are involved in a sexual relationship with one man. Although they are faithful, the women believe that the men who they are dating are faithful as well, not realizing that the men are having sex with other women. One day, the conversation arises about being monogamous.

The women are shocked to find out that their men have been having sex with other women. The women have to admit to themselves that they never asked if he was having sex with others. Women, it is extremely important to communicate with the man who you are sexually involved with because you cannot assume anything. Trust me, there are some decent men among us, and if you can accept the truth, they are willing to be honest with you.

Does He Treat You Like a Queen?

If your man is not making you feel like a queen, pay attention. He does not feel much like a king. He cannot give you something that he does not have. When a man treats you like a queen, he will not want to see you hurt. Therefore, he will forever consider your feelings before making decisions within the relationship. Your man will not stand by and let anyone talk badly about you without speaking up. He will love you unconditionally.

He will bring sunshine into your life, and he will resolve his past issues so that they will not interfere with your current relationship. Your man should not be ashamed to kiss you gently on your lips in public, if the mood hits him or wrap his arms around you. A good man respects you all the time. He will do his best to keep you satisfied (including in bed), and you in turn must do the same. Do not misunderstand me, no one is perfect. Men are human, and they will make mistakes. But a real man will apologize when he is wrong, and he will mean it.

If You Are Paying His Bills, Tell Him to Head for the Hills

Although your man may lose his job, it is not your responsibility to take care of him. Married couples look out for each other, but it should not become a serious habit. A real man will not want you to pay his car note, cell phone, and mortgage, nor should you buy him gas. It is the man's responsibility to do his best to find another job. Too often women step up to the plate, and they start taking on the role of the man.

At times, it may be difficult for a man to find another job because of the way the economy has been. However, you should be able to tell the difference between a man who is looking for employment and one who just does not want to work at all. If he is sleeping in late, does not read the unemployment section, is home when you get in from work, and dinner is not cooked, pay attention to the red flags: he is not interested in finding a job.

Is He Ready for Marriage and the Baby Carriage?

If you are trying to figure out when he will be ready for marriage, he is not the man for you. Women, a man should be hoping that you are going to marry him. Men set their own time as to when they plan to get married. Pay attention. He will not make a commitment until he is ready. Several men told me that when they were dating, they knew that they were not going to marry the woman because they were looking for a woman who was not desperate.

Although they were having sex, it did not matter. She was just not the right one for marriage. Eric said that he got turned off when his girlfriend asked him about marriage and having babies. He said, "I ended the relationship by not answering the phone when she called, I stopped calling her, and I was busy when she came by the job to visit me."

According to Eric, she finally got the message, and the relationship ended. Six months later, he dated another woman, and they got married. It has been three years since their wedding. Now they are planning to have children together. Women, if you have to beg and cry to get him to say "I do," he is not the one. Pay attention. Does this sound familiar to you?

Can You Be Friends with Your Ex?

Nothing is more difficult than to walk away from someone who you have spent years living with, especially if the two of you met on the job, still work together, or have mutual friends. After the relationship ends, the friendship needs to end as well. Now, that does not mean you should be disrespectful to your ex. However, it is futile to hold onto a friendship when the intimacy between you two has died, and you are still angry about the breakup.

The biggest challenge is that you will see each other at parties, and you will have to accept that he is dating someone else. If you know that you have not fallen out of love with your ex, it may be best to avoid spending time around him. But you can still spend time with your friends at a different event. Use your gifts that God has given you, and save your energy to find a new companion and become his best friend. Real love is waiting for you.

Feeling Used and Abused

It is common for some women to feel used and abused by their man. It becomes a love/hate relationship that can be damaging in the long run. Women who have confidence in themselves will not let a man continue using them once they have been made aware that they are being used. You are fantastic, sis, and you should never feel insecure again.

Slow Down On Giving Up the Honey

Let's face it; in this society some women have no problem giving up their cookie to a man on the first date. Slow it down. Give yourself enough time to be sure that he is the one you want to have sex with and give your heart to. Stop letting him come to your house in the middle of the night, breaking your sleep, and leaving you so tied that you cannot even function at work. A good man will not want to disturb your rest every night.

Don't Do Anything that You Can't Get Into

He still wants to have sex with you, but he cannot get an erection. So you become frustrated, but you don't discuss your feelings. You do not want to rock the boat. You are afraid that he will get upset, and you refuse to be alone. Suddenly, you start questioning yourself and wondering if your weight is the reason he cannot get it up.

Psychological conditions, such as depression, anxiety, and poor communication or conflict with one's partner can contribute to erectile dysfunction. If this problem exists in your relationship, it is important to have an honest conversation with your soul mate. Approach this matter in a gentle, kind, and respectful manner. There are a lot of sex therapists available to assist with this issue.

Accept Only the Best

Every relationship will have some conflict. However, learning how to solve conflict is very important in a relationship so that you will not end up with negative results. Women, don't settle for second best. I know this is easier said than done. But if you truly love yourself, you need to do what is best for you. When you settle for less, it shows that you don't believe that there is a better man out there waiting to sweep you of your feet.

Do what you have to do in order to experience the kind of love that you have dreamed of for years. Men are smart, and they know exactly what to say to perk up your ears. If he is constantly telling you how wonderful you are, but he is not showing any action, then he is only giving you lip service. Remember, actions speak louder than words. Tell him to put up or shut up.

Stop Being Desperate

A desperate woman gets way ahead of herself. She makes all the plans, lays out his clothes, makes restaurant reservations, finds his lost keys, picks up his dirty underwear, dates for about a month, and has sex too quickly. She picks out the engagement ring, puts the wedding gown on layaway without discussing it with him, eats the same foods he eats, and has completely lost her own identity.

Be aware, men do not marry desperate women unless they have a motive. Put your foot on the break and slow down the car, because you think that he is happy with your actions. Women, pay attention. You are going a little overboard. It turns men of. Men are impressed with self-sufficient, confident, strong, and intelligent women. A real man is attracted to women who know what they want and find a way to get it.

Let Him Do the Calling

If you have not dated in years, let me educate you on the calling process. Women, do not call men after the first date. He should be calling you. Usually, if a man is interested in taking you out on another date, he will make every effort to get in contact with you. You should not be wondering if he is going to call you.

He should be wondering if you are going to accept his call. You are a jewel. Stop taking the lead. Let him take the next step. Men who claim to be too busy to call you are not interested in you. When a man is in love, he finds the time to call, and he keeps his word. He will try not to disappoint you. If weeks or a month have passed, and you still have not heard from him, keep on moving. Don't let any grass grow under your feet. Beautiful women, your prince is out there waiting for you.

Stop Signing Up with Men who Have Nothing to Offer

Della is a forty-two-year-old woman with long curly black hair and light skin. She is five-three and has hazel eyes. Sister to a well-known millionaire, Della grew up in an environment surrounded by positive influence. She attended one of the best schools in the state. We became friends while working on our master's degree. Later, she went to Yale University where she received her Ph.D. One day, we decided to drive to Baltimore Inner Harbor after class.

I noticed that Della was not her cheerful self. So I asked her what was wrong. She admitted that her husband of five years was found by her fifteen-year- old son in her bedroom with the next-door neighbor's wife having sex. Trying not to look surprised, and fighting to keep my heart from jumping out of my chest, somehow I kept a straight face, and I just listened. She wouldn't admit that the red flags were there in the beginning of their relationship.

She was so attracted to Arnold because he was handsome and said all the right things. You know what I mean: "I love you, you are so pretty, you smell so good, you are the one for me, you are the only one, no one makes me feel like you do, and I am never going to let you go." Now don't misunderstand me, all this is fine, well, and good to say to a woman as long as there is some action and true love behind those words. This was Arnold's first marriage.

He didn't have a job, and his parents were paying his rent. He was forty-four years old. Della taught Arnold how to cook, clean, mow the lawn, wash clothes, and paint. She allowed him to drive her second car, a 2007 Mercedes, and she bought the gas. Della's parents raised her well. She started working a summer job at the age of fourteen, had chores at home to complete, washed her own clothes, bought her own car after college, and did not have a cosigner when she purchased her home.

Della was an independent, self-sufficient woman with a lot of knowledge about how a man should treat a woman. But she had always been stuck with men who said they were trying to get it together. She looked at men's potential instead of realizing there was no plan to put things in action. Bottom line, she taught him everything he knows.

They were friends. Each year, they took vacations together, and they had keys to each other's house. Della was in a rage after telling me this story. I had to admit to her that I was shocked. She had me believing that this man was the best thing since sliced bread. The next day, she canceled all his credit cards, changed the bank account number, got new keys for the house and the Mercedes, left his clothes on the deck, and had the police ready to escort him of her property when he woke up from a long nap.

Women, get out while you can before you end up being homeless. Bad boys always have a plan B. They can leave town within a moment's notice. It may seem hard to find a quality man in today's society, but they do exist. Hold out for a real man, and not just any man. A good man is one who is going to be open and honest. He will try not to let you down, and he will let you know if he is ready for a true commitment or not.

Is He Chipping Away at Your Healthy Self-esteem?

After interviewing several women, one of them told me that she was dating the same man for seven years. Everything was going along just fine. She owned her home, and he was living in an apartment. She was doing her own thing and so was he. Although she was working a lot of hours, she always spent quality time with her boyfriend. It never seemed to be an issue for either of them. They decided to move in with each other.

Therefore, she sold her house. It was a really nice home in a quiet community. She made the decision to save the profits to make a down payment on a new house that would be in both of their names. Later, they got engaged, and they moved into their new home. On the day of the closing, he was forty-five minutes late. When he arrived, he looked really depress and at a distance. She asked him why he was late. He said that he got tied up at work. Come to find out, he was off that day because she had already called his job. Red flag.

Once the papers were all signed, the broker handed him the keys, and they left the building. She drove to the new house, and he was nowhere to be found. She waited one hour outside until he arrived. She was so upset with him. She asked,

"Where were you?" He made up an excuse that was satisfying to her at the time.

Living in the new home for a few months, she got pregnant by him. Sharing the information that she was pregnant was not good news to him. He said, "I am not ready to have children." She was extremely disappointed. Suddenly, his patterns changed. He was coming home late and wouldn't answer his cell phone. At some point, he complained about her appearance. He said, "Why can't your hair grow?"

You are getting too dark, you are gaining a lot of weight, and your feet are too big." Before long, she was starting to feel unworthy of him. She would tell herself that she was overweight and too dark, and she had big feet. Her self-esteem was in the basement. Their sexual relationship was nonexistent. She found out that he had been seeing a woman that is light skin has small feet and slim.

She loss the home, and she had to file for bankruptcy because he left her for the other woman. He has not been a good father, and she got her first child support check a year ago. Their son is five years old now. As of today, her ex-boyfriend is living with the other woman, and the two of them bought a house together not far from where she was living with her mother. Every day on her way to work, she used to drive past her ex-boyfriend's home. His car would be parked in the driveway. One day, she got sick and vomited on a lady sitting next to her on the bus. Finally, she could not stand seeing his car anymore. She moved out of the area.

Currently, she is renting a town house in Baltimore, Maryland. She wants to own a home again. All the red flags were waving in the wind, but she kept pushing them down because she was hoping that she could change her boyfriend's bad behavior. No one can change anyone but themselves. Women, stop trying to change men. Be mindful. All men do not cheat. Women want men who are self-confident, trust their own judgment, and believe in their own decision-making abilities. There is a reliable man waiting for you.

Free Your Mind

Often times women get trapped within their own mind. After the relationship is actually over, women continue talking to their friends and family members about how terrible the man was to them. The situation starts controlling them. Their mind begins to fill with a lot of unnecessary junk. When women regress to an earlier bad relationship, they are trying to avoid the anxieties of the present.

Gain control of yourself, no matter how painful your emotions may be at this point. After you clean out all the garbage, you will find an appropriate way of thinking about your life. You will soon be able to have a healthier and more loving relationship with another man who is worthy of you. Don't be critical of all men. Remember, all men are not the same. Focus more on self-growth than self-pity. Make every effort to be aware of your thinking. Eventually, you will make healthier choices and restructure your mind.

Know When to Be Quiet

When a woman is silent, men will follow their own thought process. Once the man realizes that you won't interrupt him, he will respond to you in a respectful manner. Strive to develop good listening skills in order to communicate well with your mate.

Suffering in Silence

Nothing surprised me more than finding out that a woman had been suffering in silence. I interviewed a woman, and she shared with me that she had to smile when she really wanted to cry. Laura was dating a man for seven days. They met at a play in Washington DC. Their seats were next to each other. At break time, he struck up a conversation, and they exchanged phone numbers.

He called her every day by five o'clock in the morning. He invited her to dinner at his place six months later. All he talked about was how wonderful his house was, how much he paid for it, and his large bank account. Dinner was good, and the dessert he made was fantastic. After he had three drinks, he offered her a drink. She accepted. Realizing it was getting late, she asked him if she could spend the night. She did not pay attention to the fact that he was stuck on himself. His handsome face and brown eyes turned her on. Then, the heels came of, and she undressed in front of him.

They attempted to have sex on the couch. Not knowing what to expect, he pulled out his penis, and it looked like a hook. She could not believe her eyes. She spent three hours suffering in silence because she was afraid to speak up and get the hell out of there. As he tried to insert his penis into her vagina, she became annoyed and frustrated. Finally, she told him that she had to go to the bathroom, which was down a long hall near a side door. She eased her slip of the couch, but she could not find her underwear or bra. Sliding the door open, she proceeded down the stairs of the condo. Somehow, her slip got caught on a sharp edge, and it ripped.

She was naked. Her car was parked under bright lights. As she bent over to get the emergency key from under the side of her car, a dog came and licked her butt. She screamed, and a man opened his door. She ran two blocks down the street with no clothes on. As the saying goes, everything that shines is not gold.

Benefit of Therapy

Several of the roles women take on in life are those they have been told they must play. Some couples seek therapy because they are having a difficult time resolving conflict within their relationships. Therapy can provide a comfortable and safe environment so that one's life decisions can be evaluated. Mina is a thirty-two-year-old African American woman who relied on her husband to provide for her.

She had not worked since her marriage to Jonathan eleven years ago. Mina and Jonathan were doing poorly in their marriage, and they agreed on therapy in order to explore options to remain married and not divorce. Because she did not want to share their problems with anyone other than the therapist, she had no support from family or friends. Mina valued her privacy. She certainly did not want anyone knowing that her husband was having sex with other members of her family. It was too embarrassing her.

The therapist made Mina feel nonjudgmental, which allowed her to decide to leave her husband who had been having multiple affairs with her cousin, stepmother, and older sister. He expected Mina to keep quiet about his affairs. He threatened to cut her of sexually and stop paying the bills if she told anyone about his affairs. He was fixated on other women.

Jonathan was not expecting Mina to open up to the therapist about his affairs. However, Mina got the strength to make an intelligent decision. Jonathan assumed that the therapy sessions would be about Mina not helping around the house. After she left her husband, she took a job in a new city as a secretary, and she had her own office. She enrolled in college part-time to become a relationship therapist. Mina completed her master's degree, remarried a wonderful man, and she now owns her own business and has two children. Mina is living a healthy and satisfying life.

Flooding with Anxiety

Being used can trigger an anxiety attack. You feel threatened, which may feel unavoidable. After a breakup, you have to make every attempt to cope with the negative feeling of being alone or unloved. Every effort needs to be made to deal with the anxiety to prevent it from controlling you. You have to control it before it becomes excessive. One woman told me that she walked in on her husband having sex with a girl who was ten years younger than he was.

Her heart began to race fast, stomachaches developed, and she felt a shortness of breath. The anxiety started to affect her concentration at work, her mood changed, and she had difficulty developing a new relationship for fear of being cheated on again. When she would visualize them on the basement floor, it triggered an anxiety attack. Without treatment, anxiety will cripple you from functioning in your daily life.

Stupid Behaviors, but Planning to Recover

The number-one thing you need to do is figure out why you remain in an abusive relationship. Do you have concerns that you will not be able to pay your bills, such as your mortgage, buy food, or pay your car note? Are you afraid that he will marry someone else? Changing your thoughts will help you learn to focus more on positive things. After a while, you will be on the road to recovery.

When individuals become overwhelmed with grief, they have trouble thinking in ways that can calm their emotions. Face your problems head-on, and do what is necessary to help yourself recover. I have had to tell myself over and over again that forgiveness is the first step. I have battled with forgiving people in my personal life. If someone has done you wrong, you may not want to spend time with him. However, you must forgive him. The battle is not yours; it belongs to God. Focus more on accepting responsibility for your own decisions, and refuse to place unnecessary blame on the man.

When You Learn from the Past, You Make Better Choices in the Future

We have been told that if we live in the past, we will die every day. However, it is only natural to look back at the past in order to move forward. We learn from looking backward so that we don't repeat bad habits, and we can live life to the fullest.

Feeling Inadequate

If he is pushing you to move into a position that you are neither ready for nor interested in, pay attention. For a time in your life, you may feel shame. Although you are working, have a great retirement plan, own your home, drive a nice car, you may feel that you are not growing. At some point, you look over at your boyfriend, and you notice that he is climbing up the corporate ladder, but you think that he is wondering to himself, *Why in heaven am I still dating this woman after so many years?*

Then you continue to watch your friend and her boyfriend growing together. You feel bad because you are not going anywhere in your career. A true man will make an effort to help you deal with your issues, he will be supportive, and he will not judge you or walk out of the relationship. If the man who you are dating walks out, you will find a way to focus again on you. It is so simple when your mind is clear. Life can be strange at times, but do not be afraid. God will look out for you in spite of your enemies.

Struggling to Hide Low Self-esteem

Low self-esteem can pull you down so low that you will perform poorly in your everyday life. Low self-esteem will make you respond negatively when your relationship with a man ends. Low self-esteem can be the result of your parents calling you names, such as stupid, dumb, no good, and lazy.

However, self-esteem is affected more when you get involved with a man who is verbally abusive. There is an abusive man in every neighborhood. Unfortunately, he does not glow in the dark. Low self-esteem can cause you to become a people pleaser, and other people's opinions will dictate your whole life.

Praise can benefit women. It makes them feel satisfied, appreciated, and happy. Self-esteem is the essence of living with positivity and responding to life's difficulties in a realistic way. Low self-esteem usually leads to self-dissatisfaction, which robs a person of self-confidence and causes irrational thinking. Low self-esteem affects emotions and can lead to major depression.

There are some strong independent women who suffer from low self-esteem, and they are not even aware of it. Women, you are precious. Love yourself no matter how big or small your nose is, if you have long or short hair, if you have dark or light skin, if you are overweight or slim, or if you are short or tall. Believe that you are who God wants you to be. Start with loving yourself on the inside and out immediately. Then you will learn to love others.

Some common causes of low self-esteem are: negligence: children who were raised in an environment where there was a lack of love and affection find it difficult to trust others; criticism: reminding children that they are never going to be successful results in depression, and the child lack self confidence which affects their adult life. .

Moving Forward as a Single Parent

On this day, we are where we need to be for the moment. If you are now the head of the household, you probably do not have the privilege of considering whether or not to work. Gainful employment is most likely an economic necessity. Being able to wake up each day in your right mind is a blessing. Praise God that you are allowed to provide for your family.

Too often, women are too dependent on men. Once the man leaves the relationship, the woman blames him for not providing for the family. To be honest with you, it is both parents' responsibility. Do not give up on yourself. You will survive. At no point will you starve. Reach back and grab the strength and confidence that you had when you were single and free. Women who come from well-structured, supportive, and communicative families tend to develop respect for their friends, family, and strangers. Plus, they are caring and able to give and receive love.

He Changed His Mind about Being Married

Terrible things happen to all people. If we blame other people all the time for our own choices or mistakes, it is a sure sign of low self-esteem. Eventually, we feel helpless, useless, and worthless. Take a look at your life. Ask yourself who is to blame for where you are in life today. When terrible things happen, do not internalize the pain. Talk to a true friend, family member, or therapist.

Divorce can have a long-term effect on a woman's life. Be patient and true to yourself. Have the courage and break the silence in order to receive the love and support that you need at this difficult time. Sharing your hurt will arm you with positive thinking, which will help you feel better about life in general, and it will build up your self-esteem. Bottom line, anyone can get a good hug, but you want to feel the love when a man holds you.

Never Give Up on Yourself

You have to believe that all men are not out to use you. Even with the frustration you are feeling, move forward toward the goal line. You may be scared to death, as your world around you has begun to change. You can't sit in front of the television all day and night eating popcorn and candy and drinking wine. Get up right now, free yourself, dream big, and strive to achieve a better life with someone else later in the future. God created man and woman to be together. He will give you the desirers of your heart.

All you have to do is be yourself. Avoid sympathy. When friends sympathize with you from your deep hole, they end up jumping in with you and experiencing your distress. But when they empathize with you, they help you get centered in a clear space, and from there they can throw you a strong rope to help you climb out of the deep hole.

Are you angry with yourself? Do you wish you made a different choice in men? Are you still having the stomachaches since he left? For a while, things may get worse before they get better. Stop trying so hard to get even with him. Just take one day at a time. It is a fact that time heals all wounds.

Preparing Dinner

It is early evening, and you are preparing dinner. The phone rings, and it is your ex. After speaking to him, you start thinking about how hard it is to find a lasting relationship with a man that will love you. Then you flash back to your parents, all the issues you had, and to the unhealthy patterns they instilled in you. You become sad, but then you start to cry and laugh about the same time. This is still about the breakup with your ex.

One phone call from your ex-nothing but bad news brought up all your pain and deepest issues. Right now, block his phone number. Stop taking his calls since they seem to upset you. It is about getting you to think and feel better. Once upon a time, I used to believe if I did everything right, nothing disappointing would happen to me. I had my first child at age fifteen, and I began working at age seventeen. I had confidence, unlimited ideas, and great possibilities.

I told myself, *Live your dream, figure out a plan to start your own business, complete your education to reach your goals, and you will live a healthy life.* I got married, and I had two more children. For several years, I was happily married, but things changed. As in life, they sometimes do. A number of unwanted and undeserved events occurred in my life. Within a few years, several of my long- term friendships came to an end, and they were all hurtful. I had worked several jobs for a while to provide for my children that were not satisfying to me. Opportunities that I had been excited about turned boring. Suddenly, nothing seemed clear anymore.

People who I counted on to be there had vanished. I divorced in 1987, and my mom died in 1993. Happiness was gone. The most frightening thing of all was that I had to hide my feelings from the world. I was proud of myself for being able to work two jobs. I was always inspired by being independent.

My own life reflected this same attempt at superwoman multitasking. Everyone has had to face obstacles in their life, but you cannot let those things get in the way of your dreams. Life goes on, and it is so beautiful to be alive. I have always had a fear of reaching the end of my life, and feeling disappointed in me for not publishing this book.

Check Him Out First

Protection is the number-one reason to check a man out before you decide to go on a date. Going out with a stranger can be dangerous. In today's society, women are meeting men on the Internet and dating services. It has been found that men have lied about being single. Women have gone out with men who they know nothing about but only what they have been told. He could be married or a criminal. Certainly, people think that they can recognize a man who is precarious.

I have known people who have married men who they have met on the Internet, and their marriage is wonderful, but the women did their homework first. Others did not. If you are looking to get into a long-term relationship, dig deeper into his background. If he does not tell you where he lives or gives you a home phone number, most likely you will be meeting his representative.

Malaine learned the hard way. A man name Alfred told her that he used to live in California. Alfred said that he was single, had no children, and moved to Texas to be close to his parents. After their fourth date, he invited her to his condo in a well-to-do neighborhood. Driving through the underground parking garage, she noticed two cars with their headlights on, and he drove straight in front of them. Then Alfred turned to the left and parked the car. As they entered the elevator, a man's hand caught the door before it closed. Malaine was standing in the corner, and Alfred was close by.

The two men pushed the button for the second floor, and Malanie and Alfred got off on the first floor. As they were walking towards his condo apartment, one man grabbed her by the neck from behind, another hand cuffed her, and Alfred held a 38 gun to her head and told her to keep her mouth shut. They led her into the condo, ripped off her clothes, punched her in the right eye, forced alcohol down her throat, and raped her repeatedly. The horrible news was reported to the police. After the investigation, the men were arrested.

She learned later that her own brother planned the rape because he owed money to the two men, who were drug dealers. Come to find out, Alfred was from California, he had four children, and he murdered his wife because she found out that he had been raping women in the neighborhood. He was facing rape and murder charges. He left the area after he got out on bond.

View the relationship as something new. Find out as much as you can about the man before going to his apartment.

Signs of a Needy Person

As women, we tend to have a need to receive and give attention to those we love. Some of us need more attention than others. When you find yourself seeking out attention every moment of the day, you are too needy. I am not referring to receiving praise from your boss at work or from a family member at home.

I am speaking to those of us who constantly question men about how they feel about them. Hearing someone tell you how great you are is fine, but do not expect them to overdo it, even if it makes you feel good. You should feel comfortable with yourself whether or not you get praise. Just remember, you are one of a kind. There is no one like you.

Shake Yourself Loose from that Man

Have confidence in your ability to get through life. Although it may hurt for a while, life goes on. Consider it a new beginning. It takes a lot of nerve to get out of an abusive relationship. Recognize that you have taken your freedom back, and stay true to yourself. You have freed yourself from being confined in a tight space. Go have fun with your friends, and refocus on things that are positive. Try to help others.

Helping others takes your mind of yourself. Let your obstacles encourage you to reach your next level. Keep growing into a more upbeat person. You have a heart of gold, and it is filled with so much love. Do not suppress your feelings when the right man gets close. Watch your body language.

Ask God to help you make the right choices in life. With him on your side, you can never go wrong. The greatest people in the world are those who do not know it, and I am telling you that you are one of those great people. In life, God gives grace to the humble but resists the proud. Clothing does not create the woman; it reflects the lady within.

When God birthed you, he did the world a huge favor. You are a divine vessel of God. As you continue to walk the earth and live this life, guard your heart and mind against all negative and unhealthy relationships. You may not be superwoman, but you certainly are a terrific woman. Start to empower others by seeking their assistance.

Make every effort to live a balanced life in spite of your obligations. Do not let work and responsibility rule your life. You must have a balance between work and play time. Get as much rest as possible. If it is a summer or spring day, go outside, let your hair down, take your shoes of, walk around the block, and shake yourself loose until all the baggage falls of. Wait with bated breathe for your new man to come along. I am your biggest fan. I want nothing but the best for you.

Sex Is the Icing, But It Is Not the Cake

One thing is for sure, love takes time, whether it is with a friend or during courtship. Being happy already will allow a man to add to your happiness. In life, there are a few people who find true love, and others do not believe that it exists. Hold on tight, relax, enjoy, trust your feelings, listen to your heart, and believe that you are lovable and deserve love from a man. Someone special is waiting for you. Everyone has done something that they truly regret, whether it is good or bad. Do not settle for sex. It is only the icing.

You deserve the whole cake. He may have been everything that you dreamed of in a man: handsome, well built inside and out, knowledgeable, sexy, and outgoing. But something happened to change his or your mind about the relationship. When God orders our steps in his will, he does some strange things that are normally in our favor. God holds no good thing from us. You need to ask yourself if you chose him as your mate or if you sought God for a mate. Trust me, you are worth waiting for. You are precious. Any man would be fortunate to have you as a mate. The icing can melt, but the cake will last.

Tackle the Insecurities Head-on

Are you feeling that you do not deserve true love? Are you beating yourself up over your decision to leave or wanting to leave? Are you promising yourself never to get burned again? Are you thinking that it is your fault that he left? Do you believe that all men are the same? Are you wondering if you will ever find love again? Have you given up on having a healthy relationship with a good man? Are you willing to settle for less? Are you afraid to be alone?

Are you rushing into another relationship before you have recovered from your last relationship? Face your fears before entering into another relationship. If you do not deal with your issues, you will take those same problems into a new relationship, and you will repeat bad habits. You must take some time to get to know yourself. Take some time for you. Slow down and wait on your good man to come along.. You are everything that a man wants in a woman. Ask God for guidance. Going through the grieving process is normal. Just remember, beauty is not just on the outside. What matters is on the inside. A good-looking man may be the worst thing in a pair of pants? You will have your soul mate. When you get into a healthy relationship with a man, be honest with him up front. Tell him upfront your expectations, share your moral and values with him. Be honest with him. Do not lead him to believe that you are someone else. Be yourself at all times. Never doubt yourself. Having a strong spiritual base is important.

Feeling insecure will rob you of your full potential in life. Strive to reach your highest level, live up to your own standards in life, learn from your mistakes, love yourself and keep moving forward. Those men that are willing to engage in unconditional love are in society, and they are looking for a woman like you.